Stu,

with them

MML
7. 11. 23

SURVIVING LARKIN

Will Kemp has won various competitions (e.g. Cinnamon Short Story Prize, Keats-Shelley Prize), been highly
commended in others (e.g. Aesthetica Award, Wordsmiths Competition) and had work published in various magazines (e.g. *Ambit*, *Dreamcatcher*, *Interpreters
House*). He teaches Creative Writing at York University
and judges the Keats-Shelley Prize.

Surviving Larkin

WILL KEMP

VP

Valley Press

First published in 2023 by Valley Press
Woodend, The Crescent, Scarborough, YO11 2PW
www.valleypressuk.com

ISBN 978-1-915606-08-2
Cat. no. VP0215

Original cover photograph by Hildgrim.
Cover and text design by Jamie McGarry.
Editing by Jo Haywood.

Printed and bound in Great Britain by Clays Ltd.

Contents

for Vini

with thanks for the music

It is not the strongest species that survive, not the most intelligent, but the ones most responsive to change.

– Charles Darwin

Hell in the Afternoon

Vines pervaded the lattice linking the villa to the security gate, and trailed down to the pink of the bougainvillea by the pool overlooking the surrounding campagna. The heat of the day was spent but the baked flagstones still hot underfoot as his tiny hands tugged her over the frazzled lawn towards the blazing blue.

"Swim," he squeaked, a word unknown to him at the start of the holiday.

"Shhh."

"Swim," he repeated, as if it were now the only one he knew.

Mia lifted her nappied nephew one-handed onto the grass, then set him down on the incline by the pool, the foam snake and inflatable yellow duck still afloat from the day before. She slipped out of her white bath robe, letting it slump on the paving stones, then walked to the diving board and adjusted her black bikini. Not her colour really, and too sharp a contrast with her skin, though it had seemed just the thing during that half-cut shopping spree after A-levels.

Showtime. One step and she leapt to water-bomb the stillness for maximum splash effect, then swam underwater towards the shallow end to pop up like a dolphin and spout a jet of water at him.

He'd already stood up to watch, body writhing in delight at the sloshing before him, dumpy legs stamping up and down at the one-girl show.

"More," he giggled, clapping, cherub face squished in delight. "More!"

She began her routine, showing off. The back flip. The sideways fall. The walk-like-an-Egyptian walk. An idiotic head thrust through the inflatable. The headstand. The handstand. The handstand walk upside down with legs bicycling in the air. A length of back crawl. One of butterfly. And then the finale – the captain's last salute while walking down the slope to the deep end until fully submerged.

He stood at the pool's edge with hands between crossed legs, as if desperate for a wee, barely able to contain himself at the performing seal she'd become.

Time for some audience participation. Slinking to the shallow end, she handed him the foam snake. He took it in both hands and bonked her on the head. She lolled her tongue and pulled a *Tom and Jerry* face spinning with stars.

"Aaaagggh!" she cried, falling over with an exaggerated crash to shower him with spray.

"More," he gushed, sopping, then started to bash the water with the snake.

This time she dived back into the deep end, swimming close to the bottom in a figure of eight, spinning like a metal hook at the end of a fishing line, dark blue shadow in close pursuit. Something for him to marvel at. She hadn't been captain of swimming for nothing.

At last she returned to the shallow end, desperate for air. But this time there was no clapping, no giggling, no bashing. Just the aimless drift of the snake without its tormentor. Robbie was nowhere to be seen.

Her eyes scoured the borders. Perhaps he was playing a game, concealed behind a bush or tree. He'd had ample time to take cover – she could hold her breath for over a minute. She scanned the shrubs again, expecting to spot him in his usual hiding pose: white nappy protruding from the side of a bush, eyes shut tight in the belief that nobody could see him if he couldn't see them. But there was nothing.

Perhaps Sara had come and taken him in... No, Mia would have seen her, she'd have stayed. Besides, not enough time had passed... And then the unthinkable: had he fallen in?

Mia froze. Looked around, trying to see through the glassy surface of the water, panic pooling in her. It gleamed with unhelpful reflections of sky. But to her left was a little pink and white bundle, at the bottom of the deep end.

She hit the water hard, upending herself, not even taking a breath, plunging down to him – but without the power, the velocity, she needed to get to him that second, that very second.

She heaved her arms through the water in a powerful breaststroke swipe, and another, surging towards him. Placed a foot by his side, one hand under his legs and the other to support his head, then scooped him up and sprang towards the surface, extending her arms as if making an offering to the sky, giving him an extra split-second in which to breathe, to live... Oh please God, let him live – take her life, anything – but let *him* live...

As she surfaced, gravity dragged her down. Her legs dangled uselessly in the water. She kicked upwards to keep him aloft, his body suddenly colossally heavy.

Her head resurfaced, then submersed involuntarily again, making her swallow chlorinated water. She had to see him.

She kicked again, gaining enough elevation to tread water, and looked at him. His mouth was shut, face running with water and trembling, blue eyes open wide and blinking like a doll's.

Oh thank God. He was alive. The sweet, darling boy was still alive.

Struggling to hold him aloft, her legs struck out towards the slope until she could gain enough of a foothold to stand on tip-toe.

"Robbie," she asserted, walking into the shallow end. "Listen to me. Are you OK?"

His head turned towards her in the slow manner of a robot. He was in shock, his life still in the balance. What if he choked on a mouthful of water? Or had brain damage?

Mia held him under his arms and tipped him slightly to one side. He spluttered, then looked on with a blank stare, saliva dribbling down his chin, body shivering.

She folded him into her firmly, so his head rested over her shoulder, then arched backwards to tip his little head towards the water. There was a guttural cough then a swash of excess fluid.

Leaning forward, she brought him back in front of her, watching him in thankful disbelief he hadn't cried or opened his mouth underwater. Nobody could have taught him that – yet that was what he'd done – through some instinctive, primeval life force.

She kissed him on the forehead. The left cheek. The right cheek. Held him into her. Then out to study his face, unable to contain the forlorn look breaking over her own. His eyes shut and his mouth showed two regimented rows of milk teeth as if mirroring hers, then bawled to burst the lazy calm of the late afternoon.

Mia nursed him back into her with the pained joy of mothers holding sons returned from war, convulsing with tears. And somehow laughing too, at the thought of the future story that her kiss was enough to make anyone cry.

"There, Robbie," she soothed, voice faltering, kissing him again, right hand sweeping his back as she bobbed him up and down. "Good boy. Good boy. Good boy."

Sara must have heard the cry, because in no time she was marching across the lawn in her bath robe, blonde hair in a bun. She looked pretty, but pretty non-plussed too. Mia dipped her face in the water to wash away the tears, then re-entered the atmosphere with a sheepish look, chest tightening.

"Did he fall in?" Sara demanded with a big sister glare, arms outstretched to take him back.

Mia handed him over, not knowing what to say. Why hadn't she prepared a believable story?

"Well," she stalled, looking away at a puddle nearby. "I was just mucking about…"

Mia's brittle voice caught in her throat as she gazed back at the mother and child above, the natural order restored. Her face started to crumple again.

"Don't lie," Sara snapped. "What happened?"

She was right. It was no time for lies. And Mia had always been a useless liar. And he was soaked. Of course he'd fallen in.

"Yes," she burbled, caving in. "He did. I'm sorry."

Sara's look slapped her little squirt of a sister across the face. She tutted then rolled her eyes skyward, head shaking.

"I was playing in the shallow end," Mia bleated, looking across the grass, cooking up some scenario so Sara would never have to picture him plopping headlong into the deep end.

The young mother turned without waiting for Mia to finish and stomped back across the grass, whisking Robbie away indoors. Out of harm's way.

Mia remained standing in the pool. The water was still lapping against the sides from the earlier commotion, as if a water polo match had just finished. A flotsam of playthings drifted about at random, the smile on the inflatable duck broad like a circus clown's.

She placed her forearms on the side and bowed her head onto them, drained, framing a view of the luminous blue below – possibly even the spot where Robbie tumbled in, sank, brushed the slope then rolled away before coming to rest, bewildered, for what must have seemed an eternity.

Her heart jolted. How close to death he'd come. She thought of the difficult arrangements, the scenes too – the child's coffin, the procession, Sara clasping Steve in horrific grief. The end of everything. Her mouth contorted again, emitting a low caterwaul, face streaming, body shaking.

It had seemed so right to come. A tan before uni. Put *au pair* on her empty CV. Meet some Brutus at the market with its aroma of oranges and peppers, then text her friends to make them jealous as hell. And look after Robbie every now and then to give Sara some me-time. Though the last few minutes had been as far away from *looking after* him as Hampshire.

She looked towards the deep end as if staring into the abyss. A watermark stated the depth as 2.2m. So nearly the recorded depth of drowning in the coroner's report; the exact distance between life and death. Not just of his life, but hers as well – because if he had died, she'd have been dead in the water too.

Her sister had entrusted her – without even thinking – with that which meant most to her, and in Mia's care, that most precious thing had nearly died.

What she'd done was unforgiveable. In ancient Greece, she'd have been banished from the kingdom. Had her feet spiked with irons. Been left to die on a mountain. And really, that was what she deserved.

And now she'd lied to her sister, and would probably do

so for the rest of her life. If only Mum were here, to hold her, tell her it'd be all right, anything, to end this maelstrom. As it was, she'd never felt more alone.

The solemn bulwark of a cloud looked down. The slow-burning sky here had seen all manner of things – legions marching north, Goths rolling south – sacking, raping, killing. And had almost witnessed another tragedy.

But then again, she couldn't have acted more quickly or effectively during those frantic seconds. And Robbie was alive. Surely that was the only thing that mattered.

She looked about her. The doused flagstones evidenced the thrashing that had taken place – no longer newly wet, but drying in the after-heat of the day. In less than ten minutes there'd be nothing left, not even a trace of water. Robbie would be dry too, wearing his tiger sleep-suit and strapped into the high-chair, drinking a carton of apple juice through a straw or dragging an orange crayon across a picture of Peter Pan. Sara would be starting to make his tea, asking if Mia would like some iced tea or a glass of wine. Everything would be entirely normal.

Mia looked at the water's settling surface, unsure whether she'd saved his life or nearly drowned him.

How to Deal with a Dark Smoke Offence

They were crossing the Ouse after the weekly abbatoir inspection when Julie sat forward, transfixed by a distant ribbon of black smoke rising above the flatscape of bare fields.

"Mark," she started, rain spotting the windscreen, "look at that."

"Look at what?"

"That dark smoke over there."

She stared at the obvious column beyond Winthorpe, then turned to him, ponytail swishing round with her incredulous look.

"Oh yeah," he nodded in his shades, flicking on the wipers.

He'd seen the smoke all right, its thread joining earth to sky, could picture too the gypsies or farmers at its base, burning tyres. They'd have started the fire knowing the smoke would soon be undetectable against the night sky and that no officer was going to investigate an incident on a Friday afternoon.

"Well?" She asked.

"Well, it doesn't look too bad to me."

"Surely we have to at least investigate?"

"Dunno. It's probably a car smash."

He could feel her brown eyes drilling through the side of his skull.

"Oh come on Mark, you know I've not done a prosecution yet."

So much for getting back to the office by five – their

colleagues gone – and asking her out for a drink under the pretext of work. What had she learnt today. What would she put in her log book. How was the day course going. Would she be riding this weekend. What bands did she like. Did she know he played guitar.

"Well?" She persisted.

His eyes skimmed the plume. Of course it was a dark smoke incident. A Ringelmann 4 without question. And he was a *chartered* Environmental Health Officer. He – they – *had* to investigate.

"Oh all right then," he relented. "Let's go and take a look."

He turned off the motorway and headed for the tornado of smoke as Julie tried to locate it on her mobile. He'd been struck by her Sandra Bullock looks and smile the day she started as a trainee, though she'd not been short of offers to go on inspections from the other young EHOs who put each other down at every turn.

"Oi Marco," Dave had broadcast across the office as they were leaving, "tell her about the time you tested the water quality at Swinton Reservoir – and turned it bright yellow for a week by putting in ten dye tablets instead of one…"

Hard alpha male laughter had broken out, leaving him red-faced. But Mark was a man with a plan; while his rivals relied on the pool car – a rusting Ford Fiesta – for site visits, he'd bought a second-hand racing green Golf GTi Convertible, spending weekends adding alloy wheels and leather seats until she was fit for a princess.

"It must be somewhere near Addlesby," she gauged, face bathed in an unearthly glow from the phone below.

"Right," he began, as the rear wheels of the tractor in front spluttered mud pies onto the road. "That gives us five minutes. Do you want to lead this or shall I?"

"Can I?" She sparkled.

Mark gazed at the contraption ahead, remembering how she'd jumped at the chance to report back from their group at last month's training session: without any notes, she'd stood before fifty colleagues to deliver her summary with an effortless clarity that put the bumbling director to shame.

He ran through the basics for her. Carcinogens. PM10s. The Clean Air Acts. That dark smoke emitted from a trade or industrial premises is a strict liability offence, so such an incident must be stopped with immediate effect. The offender could then be prosecuted with 100 per cent liability for costs. Julie watched him intently, taking it in.

"So how would you approach it?" He probed, overtaking the tractor.

She looked puzzled.

"The investigative interview," he hinted. "How would you start it? What would you say?"

"Oh, I see!" Julie laughed, slapping a flat hand against her forehead as if showing how she'd just walked into a door. "Doh!"

It was impossible not to answer her grin with his own.

"I'd… A, issue the caution," she responded, eyes closed as if reciting notes, "then B, establish who owns the land, C, take some photographs, and D… And D, ask them what they're doing?"

"Correct. Especially that last bit. Try and get them to *admit* they're burning tyres."

Julie beamed, as if about to burst into song.

God, she was stunning. If only they weren't colleagues, he might stop the car, lean over, take her face in both hands and kiss her. And she'd let that dark hair fall around her shoulders, begin unbuttoning her blouse…

"Then what?" She carried on, looking at him directly.

He'd gone blank.

"PACE," he affirmed, slowing down behind a cyclist, "what do you understand by PACE?"

"I'm sorry?"

"PACE stands for Police and Criminal Evidence. So a PACE interview is one under caution. Basically the same powers as the police. Got it?"

"Got it," she confirmed, a co-pilot in the cockpit.

What a girl. If she played for Man U the manager would never have to fret about her slacking in midfield or joining Man City.

"Good. How far to go now, do you reckon?"

She consulted the phone again, humming to herself, while he waited for the on-coming traffic to clear.

It wasn't just that she was attractive, reliable, assured. She was intelligent. Well-spoken. Sporty. Hard-working. Positive. Wholesome. Able to laugh at herself; make others laugh too. The type of girl to take home and meet his mother. The type of girl to spend easy afternoons with, walking in the park or watching *Casablanca* on the sofa. The type of girl he'd always wanted.

"According to this," she pondered, looking for road signs, "we should come to a left turn soon."

He looked at the ditches lining the road, the gnarled oaks punctuating the threadbare hedges. Tiny green shoots would soon be furring the fields.

"There it is," she asserted, pointing to a road sign a few hundred yards ahead. "That must be it."

"One more thing," he added, "do you know what a Ringelmann Chart is?"

"Hang on," she replied, bending forward to scrabble around in her handbag on the floor.

He caught a peep of her bra and the delicious olive-brown

flesh beneath her blouse.

"Ta-da!" she exclaimed, holding up the chart in triumph. "Here it is. It helps you determine how dark the smoke is."

"How?"

"Well, there are four types – Ringelmann 1, 2, 3 and 4. Ringelmann 1 is pale grey smoke, and harmless, while 4 is very dark, and toxic…"

She held the chart against the windscreen, checking the twister funnelling the sky half a mile away.

"…and that baby is definitely a Ringelmann 4."

They passed through Addlesby then turned off at a sign for Elm Tree Farm, the charmed snake of smoke towering above them, near but far at the same time.

The track was a mudbath. In no time the waxed body-work was caked in it. Worse still, each lane led to another, then onto the dead end of a pond or wood, forcing Mark to reverse precariously across deep ruts and retrace their route. The place was a maze, and the further afield they went the rougher the tracks became, juddering them back and forth.

They turned down one, the worst yet, with water-filled ruts on either side of a central hump against which the chassis was now constantly scraping.

"Me car," he muttered as the undercarriage thudded into it.

"Mark," she ventured, clutching the passenger door as the car rocked forward, "what do you think I should say first to start the caution?"

He tutted and shook his head, lips clenched.

"Mark?"

"For Pete's sake," he grumbled as the belly of the car grated against a stone.

He had no interest now in her precious work experience,

log book, face, bra. All that mattered was the car, dealing with this incident as quickly as possible and getting to the car-wash before it shut.

The track curved towards some red-brick barns glimpsed through the gappy hedge. She looked on, slightly pale.

"Mark, I feel a bit car-sick."

He pressed a button in silence to open her window, the farm now in plain sight straight ahead – a sturdy house with a long barn to the left, behind which a fire was raging.

"I'm sorry," she grimaced. "I don't feel well enough to do this."

He rolled his eyes toward the sunshield.

"You just take notes then. An watch an listen. An learn how to deal with a dark smoke offence."

He drove into the farmyard. A mound of tyres blazed some hundred yards to the left – palettes silhouetted against orange flames, black clouds billowing into the air like a plane crash. The car sliced through thick mud towards the fire, wheels slipping and spinning. He looked for a place to park among the silos and muck-spreaders rusting by the empty pens, then spotted a vacant storage bay in front of a retaining wall. Perfect.

The car made a beeline for the space, carving through the claggy ground, then lunged onto the bay's pad more quickly than intended before stopping. The wall in front seemed to inch upward, the red combine to the right too, as if the car tyres were deflating. He looked outside. The Golf was sinking in a quicksand of setting concrete.

They turned to each other, faces aghast with the same man-in-the-moon expression.

"Get it off," she yelled. "Get it off!"

He put the car into reverse and tried to back out. The

wheels spun, plastering the wall with a porridge of concrete. It was no use. The vehicle was going nowhere.

He slammed into first gear with a hideous scrunch and hit the accelerator, the engine revving like a frenzied chain-saw. The car sloughed forward but only seemed to settle further into the gruel.

He plunged the car back into reverse, white globs splodging out before them, then held the wheel down to the right. The vehicle started to revolve with the serenity of a display carousel at a motor show.

He tried left, then right again, backwards, forwards, only for the car to continue to pelt the farmyard with more pale grey sludge.

Then, finally, traction. So much concrete had now been threshed from the base that the rusted re-enforcement grid was exposed. He shunted the car into reverse and careered backwards, able to get enough purchase on the shutter of the bay for the car to begin sucking itself out of the bog. Thank God.

He switched off the engine and noticed a line of men standing directly in front of the inferno. All four wore blue overalls and black wellies, and glared at him with faces darkened from stoking the great fire.

He looked at Julie open-mouthed. She stared back, mirroring his expression. How on earth was he going to deal with this?

Mark had no idea. He got out and squelched into three inches of mud, at once feeling the surging heat of the fire. A white scum had formed over the mud spatter across the lower body of the Golf, which now resembled a long distance rally car. The underside would be ten times worse. He had to get it to a spray gun to prevent the base from turning to stone. But first he had to deal with the angry men.

He held out his badge towards them at arm's length.

"Mark Thomson," he announced, "Senior Environmental Health Officer, Vale of York District Council."

The men remained motionless, the whites of their eyes marked against four sooty faces like commandos ready for a night-op.

The car lock thwipped shut as Julie peered outside. What an arse he must look in his ruined trousers and shoes. He'd never hear the end of this back at base. More to the point, he still had no idea what to say to those about to lynch him. And then it came to him.

"This is your lucky day," he declared.

The blank face of the oldest man dropped to a new level of dismay.

"It dunt fukkin look like tha from where I'm standin," he smouldered.

He had a point. The would-be bay was churned up horribly, like leftover rice pudding. The left side of the combine was daubed white, as if caught in drift snow. Half the pad's concrete was now deposited across the farmyard in great splays akin to a fire extinguisher prank gone wrong.

"We've just laid tha," the man strained in exasperation, shifting to one side as if lining up a punch at full tilt.

"A dark smoke offence can carry a fine of up to twenty thousand pounds," Mark clipped in a traffic warden kind of way. "But in view of the disruption to your pad, I'm prepared not to prosecute."

The man eyeballed him, fists clenched, chest heaving, face purple under the soot.

"Believe me, this is your lucky day."

Time to leave. Mark got back into the horseradish sauce-splattered car, started the engine and began rolling it forward. He paused by the stupefied man to wind the window down.

"Now let that be a lesson to you," he warned over his shades.

The fire-starter remained rooted to the spot amid the carnage of the yard, watching stone-faced as the kid from the council drove off without waiting for a reply.

Mark expected a hurled brick to clunk against the boot of the car amid a torrent of abuse, but all he could hear was the scratching of Julie's pen in her log book.

"What's that you're writing?" He inquired, peeking sideways at her page as if cheating in an exam.

She lifted her head and turned to him with a look of uncertainty.

"How to deal with a dark smoke offence," she answered, then gave a wry smile.

"Oh."

He resumed his contemplation of the track ahead, grateful now for the strip of grass wiping concrete off the underbody of the car, then glanced down at her leg, wondering if he was still in with a chance.

The Day I Met Vini Reilly

Vini isn't exactly an international celebrity, but when he's loved, he's very very loved.

– Tony Wilson, Factory Records

I can't remember what I was doing when I heard about 9/11, but do remember the first time I heard The Durutti Column. It happened when I was sixteen, on a visit to London with a friend during the Easter holidays. Our parents understood the trip was necessary to see the plays we were doing for A-levels, but all we learnt that week was how to get served in a pub and what we saw in the sex cinemas of Soho.

Killing time one afternoon in Leicester Square, we bounced into a record shop to see what they had. And there, all around, was *the* most beautiful sound – neither rock nor classical, yet somehow both of them too – a haunting, atmospheric guitar, delicate and intricate, rising and falling, with distant vocals, piano and drums. I'd never heard anything like it before. I had to have it.

"Excuse me," I interrupted the assistant, engrossed in a magazine on the counter, "what's this you're playing?"

"Durutti Column," he grunted.

"What?"

"The Durutti Column. A guitarist called Vini Reilly and some other fella from Maaanchester."

He returned to his reading.

"And what's the record called?"

"*LC.*"

"*Elsie?*"

He looked up again, with a crooked smile.

"Naaa. *L.C.* Short for *Lotta Continua* – Latin for *the struggle goes on* or somefing like that. I'll get you the cover."

He turned to a library of record sleeves then handed me a white album cover with squiggles of red and orange watercolour. Intriguing, sensitive and different. Just like the music.

"Have they done anything else?"

"Yeah. Two albums. Just wait there."

As he went to fetch those too, I examined the track titles on the cover. 'Sketch for Dawn'. 'Portrait for Frazer'. 'Detail for Paul'. They must have gone to art school. Cool.

"Ere you go," he announced, placing the other two before me.

"I'll have all three, please," I hurried, blowing the last of my pocket money as well as the chance of seeing any more films in Soho.

And I suppose I knew even then that The Durutti were better than sex.

Time moves on and yet stands still. Twenty years pass. University follows school, girlfriends come and go, the Tories replace Labour, Labour replaces the Tories, the mullet supersedes the feather cut, and is itself superseded by any number of styles facilitated by the advent of hair gel. I eventually become a full-time town planner and part-time poet.

But during this time of change, one thing remains steadfast – the enduring brilliance of The Durutti Column. I buy every LP, then every CD, playing them over and over, never once tiring of Vini's distinctive, otherworldly sound, sure it is ahead of its time yet timeless too.

He thereby provides the soundtrack for my life. He's

there when I fall in love, when I score my first century, when I lose my virginity. There too when love breaks down, when my parents die, always understanding the loss with his poignant, stabbing guitar. And all the time I wait for the girl who will love The Durutti too.

The only scratch on the Ming vase is that I never see them in concert. But then they never did much stuff live. And Factory Records – hip and *alternative* – relied on word of mouth. So non-Manc-me never stood a chance of hearing about their gigs, and the finery of Vini's music also remained largely unknown.

But then God invents the internet (and God must exist, because how else would Vini exist?), and I discover The Durutti are playing in Manchester. Within five minutes, I've bought two tickets at £15 each and feel dizzy with excitement. At long last, twenty years after walking into that shop off Leicester Square, I am actually going to see Vini *live*.

My friend Pete drives. Pete is stocky, dependable and rosy-faced, like a favourite uncle. By day he works as an environmental scientist, by night he plays drums in a gypsy rock band. Like me therefore, he is both an environmental professional and *artiste de demain*.

I've invited him because I owe him favours and because he's a musician, so his opinion is sound and matters – matters, that is, unless he thinks Vini is crap, in which case he doesn't know anything and can get lost. Moreover, he's from Manchester – meaning he knows how to get to the venue – The Comedy Store, Deansgate Locks – and is happy to drive. This is critical because we can't be late and I need to be free to take in the object of my veneration-adoration-obsession.

Outside, the Pennine landscape of the M62 passes by in long hill hauls, with signs to Huddersfield and Halifax, views of bare moors and windswept reservoirs, the surface waters choppy under a grey sky.

It doesn't rain, but I want it to. I want Manchester to be Manchester, with storm clouds over dark mills, to be part of the melancholy that has inspired Vini's ethereal, often wistful, sound.

I feel tense but excited, like a child going to see a lion at the zoo. I hope there will be a full house, with some good-looking women – one of whom could be that special Durutti devotee – and some Durutti T-shirts on sale too so I can proclaim my allegiance to the Blessed One. And with the excitement come butterflies in my stomach in case we are late, Vini is ill or the hippie organisers have cocked up with the date.

A sign for Rochdale flits by. This is Vini country, I think, recalling that 'Les Preger's Tune' off the album *Vini Reilly* was a homage to a neighbour there who fought for the Communists during the Spanish Civil War.

I wonder what it must be like to have Vini dedicate a track to you, musing how he'd surely do exactly that if we met – because there's always been that connection between us, just the two of us, as if he'd created all that unique, divine music just for arty, sensitive me.

And I wonder how the drab houses and post-industrial dereliction massing the hills around us relate to his tracks, which often conjure autumnal mists and colours, the innocence of childhood. It is easy to think of his music as an escape, that his life too has been one more dreamed than lived.

And so to Manchester. We are four hours early. Four hours early but twenty years late. It is a Sunday afternoon, late April. There isn't much traffic, and it starts to rain. Not hard rain, but soft and slow – a steady, feathery drizzle – the same rain that created the textile industry and the pensive sadness that pervades so much of Vini's music.

The venue is deserted. We wander into a spacious hall with refurbished brick walls, a wooden floor and a giant TV at one end. There on the screen, without sound, an old man in a crumpled linen suit sits behind a drum kit talking to a diminutive figure with the guitar and haircut I recognise from the album cover of *Sex and Death*.

"My God," I murmur, "it's him."

"What – the band?" Pete jolts, as if waking from a snooze. "But there's only two of em."

"There *are* only two of them."

"Well, they'll be doing the sound check. In the main auditorium. But look at what he's doing, the guitarist – he's showing the drummer ow to play."

I look, and sure enough Vini is instructing drummer Bruce Mitchell on what Bruce surely knows best.

The image confirms the perfectionism I've always suspected, and makes me wonder if Vini is, in his own way, a control freak too – bursting into rages at bum notes, and more besides. I doubt it. The creator of such entrancing, gentle music could hardly be a total arsehole.

We sit down on a big black sofa, watching Vini's silent cameo performance. Occasionally, people pop in and out of camera shot, until there is no more movement. The sound-check must be over. The little genius might enter the hall at any second.

Sure enough, a small figure walks in at the far end towards the bar area. It is Vini Reilly.

I go cold inside. This is my chance to meet him, speak to him, but I have no idea what to say. I feel hollow, sixteen again, a gangly schoolboy freezing in front of the school honey for whom I've spent all week preparing and rehearsing a chat-up line that is now lost in the trembling moment of meeting.

But I have to see him, thank him… I may never get another chance.

What if he is heading for the gents though? What to do then? Accost him in there? Wait outside?

He stops at the end of the bar to join a stout woman and a man with a grey ponytail. They look pleased to see him and start talking. It is now or never.

I begin the long walk, in slow motion it seems, my head turning over possible lines. *I want to thank you… I just want to thank you… I just want to say how thankful I am…*

I reach the group, a yard away now from my all-time hero.

The conversation stops. Vini looks up at me like a street urchin awaiting sentence for some trivial theft. His face is gaunt and dry, its features gnarled and twisted, like a wooden sculpture – the nose Hispanic or Roman – his dimples suction-packed, the wild hair ashen. He reminds me of Keith Richards, only smaller and more unhealthy – a young waif and an old crone at the same time, the painfully thin neck extended like a tortoise's, his body a withered weed by the roadside.

"Er, hello," I rattle, extending a hand. "Can I buy you – buy you all – a coffee or something?"

"No, it's OK," he replies out the corner of his mouth, hand weak in mine, northern voice soft as the rain outside.

Vini Reilly has just spoken to me – the words so humble and warm I want to reach out and grab them before they dissolve into the air.

Silence. A horrible, awkward, deafening silence. If only I'd prepared something to say. And didn't sound so posh. And wasn't so tall. In fact I tower over Vini, looking down on the man I look up to. For the first time, I sense how threatening my height is, and want to be small.

The man with the ponytail gives me a dismissive look. But Vini and the woman seem to know this is an important rite of passage and await my next line with faces of calm understanding.

"Look," I restart at last, slouching in an attempt to reduce my height. "This is more embarrassing for me than it is for you…"

Vini continues his upward stare, mouth ajar – the dark eyes seeming to get bigger and bigger, like a cartoon owl's – as unbelievably *he* listens to *me*.

"…But I just want to thank you for all the colour and enrichment your music has put into my life – "

"No, no," the miniscule giant interrupts gently. "Thank *you* for buying the records."

The comment is genuine, and takes my breath away. I swallow hard, conscious of the need to say something, to keep the sacred flame of conversation alive.

"You see, I've been a fan for twenty years now, and well, I've never seen you live. And I'm really excited. About tonight, I mean. Because after all these years I'm going to see you live… So I really hope it goes well for you. Tonight, I mean."

The jumbled words tumble out of me then trail off.

"Thank you," he acknowledges, then resumes his moonish stare.

I pause, dumbstruck, noticing how big his veins are – or rather how thin his arms are. He has the emaciated look of a vagrant or drug addict – and maybe both – as if a cough or sneeze would be enough to blow him away. He must be ill, I think, wanting to nurse him back to health, wrap him in cotton wool.

"Excuse me, but I need to go for a fag," he confides, looking to break out of the tall circle around him.

"Yes, of course. Well, good luck tonight. And cheers."

"Cheers," Vini nods as he passes, so close I can feel the faint rush of his cigarette breath on my face.

I stay where I am, elated and dazed, like a prisoner of war blinking in disbelief at freedom; relieved too that Vini has a sweet nature and a sense of wonder – just as I always imagined. I feel I've known him all my life. And I suppose I have, really.

I ponder his words and treasure his earnest look, then think of the hundred questions I should have asked – which is his favourite album, where does he go shopping, can I buy him – them – a meal before the gig…

I turn to a bemused Pete, raising my arms aloft as if I'd just taken ten wickets.

"Pete, I've spoken to him! I've just bloody spoken to him!"

I shut my eyes in a state of rapture. I've got to have a beer to celebrate. Several in fact.

By the time we roll into the auditorium, the supporting act is finishing her set. When she does, the place empties for a drink before the main event, freeing up seats. We descend to the middle block, and like a pair of shameless vultures occupy the best seats in the house – five rows back from the main microphone.

Pete talks me through the electronics and angle of the jazz drums, and I take notes, acting the part of a journalist in case anyone challenges us for *their* seats. Nobody does, although when the place starts to refill I notice out the corner of my eye the ousted couple lamely accepting their misfortune.

Just as I'm thinking things cannot get any better, the stocky woman from earlier sits down next to me.

"Oh hello," I smile. "I met you earlier. Are you family, friend or another musician?"

"I'm Karen," she caws in the husky voice of a heavy smoker, "is partner of the last fower year."

"My God, that's amazing. Look, I'm sorry about earlier… It's embarrassing, but I'm such a big fan – "

"Oh, dunt worry, you're all righ. It appens quite a lot."

I pause, overcome by the chance to redeem myself, ask anything, get an insider's view of him.

"What's he like?" I dare.

"Pretty much as you'd think, I suppose."

"What, you mean quiet and sensitive? Wouldn't harm a fly?"

"That's it," she reflects. "An always dreamin. Could daydream for England that boy."

I gaze at the ceiling, head cocked slightly and mouth ajar in much the same way that Vini had looked at me.

"Bur he can be a right bastard. He woke up this mornin – I wor still sleepin – an said, can you think of a fish beginnin wi the letter H? So we lay there, for over an hour, tryin to think of all the fish beginnin wi H…"

Incredible. I've wondered exactly the same thing. How right I'd been all these years to picture him watching the clouds – the embodiment of DH Lawrence's view that the most precious element in life is wonder.

She explains that sometimes he stays up all night if he has a tune in his head and how, a few years ago, he was in real financial trouble after the break-up of Factory. I think of how I might help. I give her my business card and promise to help promote Vini's forthcoming gig through a DJ friend in London, throwing in an improbable offer of free town planning advice for good measure.

"Oh ta," she adds, a little taken aback.

"No, no," I reply, Vini-style. "Thank *you*."

Vini appears on stage, alone and uncertain, holding a guitar, and stumbles towards the microphone amid an ecstatic reception. He looks uncomfortable.

"This first one is for a nice man called Will I met earlier at the bar," I want him to say.

"Ello," he mumbles instead. "Thanks for comin. Hope you enjoy the music. This one's for me niece who's ere tonight. It's called 'Spasmic Fairy'."

Vini has never had the gift of track titles. In fact, I cannot think of a more unlikely rock star. But when he plays, he plays. And as he does, the audience is still, spellbound, drawn towards some other Hamelin, stupefied at how quickly his fingernails pluck notes from a guitar, as all the angels of heaven settle amongst the stage lights to adore the captivating sound rising from below.

This is the first track I've heard the Vinmeister play live, and it has been worth the wait. I wonder if he'll play anything from *LC*, or ask for someone to help out while he plays keyboards, picturing myself on stage with him, strumming an acoustic guitar. It isn't the first time I've wished I could play.

The second track is also instrumental, the third another solo partly accompanied by his *sotto* vocals. It is only with the fourth that old man Mitchell appears, to delirious applause, and begins to slap the drum intro to 'The Missing Boy' as if warding off a host of evil spirits.

As Vini delivers the virtuoso chords, steeped in light, he becomes bigger and bigger, the strap anchoring guitar to shoulder creating a lilac-blue shadow across his red shirt. My head and body move to the rhythm, transported, mouthing the words I know so well in time with his ghostly wail.

I think I'm in love with Vini. Not the love for a partner but the love for a kid brother. I see him as a puny outsider in the playground, the class nerd, picked on and bullied, a Mancunian Billy from *Kes* – someone who needs a good bath and a square meal inside… And suddenly I want to stand up and smash their heads in – the bullies I've never met – because nobody's going to come near my little Vin and hurt him.

He plays and plays, and I listen, hoping he'll do twenty tracks to make up for the missing years – a kind of royal gun salute. But in the end he looks shattered, and the band's sound descends into an untypical wall of noise. No doubt it is avant-garde, but I want him off stage in case he becomes ill or harms his chances of getting a record deal from someone in the crowd.

On the way home, I'm on a drug-free high – and struggle to take it in. A perfect day, better than I could have hoped for. Not only to have seen The Durutti live, but to have met Vini, and thanked him, sat next to his girlfriend even. They were brilliant; he was fantastic. But even if they'd been crap, they'd still have been brilliant. £15 a ticket? I'd have paid £1,500.

"I'm really pleased for yer, Will," Pete laughs, shaking his head as the street lights flash by. "I've never seen yer so happy. But yer've gotta learn guitar. Yer'd get so much owt of it."

He's probably right, but I'm not really listening. I'm looking out the window, mouth slightly open, thinking about all the different kinds of fish beginning with H.

To Die For

"Christ, it's hot," he'd drawl, lounging by the pool, and Silke would touch his hand in agreement, as if talking was too much effort in the heat, her nodding sunglasses the only perceptible movement for miles around.

The place had taken a beating from the sun that summer. The villa's lawn had dried up into an old beige carpet; the bushes looked parched and dead. The scrub of the surrounding hills repeated the scene on a larger scale, resembling a spaghetti western – a dusty, deserted place where bandits might take up positions behind the baking rocks to pick off strangers amid ricochets of small arms fire. A tinderbox waiting to go off.

Not that she minded. This was the Crete they'd come for, to explore on their own terms.

They decided to set off at noon, in T-shirts and shorts, passing the olive groves above the villa to the tune of the sloshing water bottle in Graham's rucksack. He led the way, oblivious to a man raising a tanned hand at a farm, though Silke waved back.

Gradually the path gave way to a trail marked by infrequent piles of stones in a no-man's-land of gorse and scree. After half an hour it dropped down into a sparse area of mixed fir trees, then petered out in the listless grass. Silke's eyes stung from the leachate of sweat and sun-cream that had started to run.

"Where are we?" She squinted, drawing level to look at the pocket-sized map in his hand.

"Well, we've come along here," he hesitated, tracing a finger along a dotted line that squiggled left from the villa. "But should have passed a cairn…"

She took the bottle from the rucksack, glugged a few mouthfuls then splashed some water around her eyes.

"We've been on a sheep trail," he realised. "Must have missed the footpath."

God he was a handsome man, with that gaunt face and dark hair – more French-looking than English – and as intelligent as a doctor should be; "good breeding stock" as her mother had once noted.

She patted her face with a tissue then inspected the map. The villa was half an inch from the entrance to the gorge but there was no scale to indicate the distance between the two points, no contours either to demarcate the terrain, just a photograph of the clear stream at the bottom of the valley.

"OK," she accepted, "so which way now?"

He stood with hands on hips, looking uphill at the wild oleander and Corsican pines, then pointed to a blue line curving right like the top of an *r*.

"See this stream?" He asked. "If we head north, we must come to it at some point. We can then follow it into the gorge, and join the walk."

"Come on, then," she agreed, "let's go."

The walk had been his idea, to escape the heat trapped in the bottom of the valley. A shortcut to the gorge, then head down to Agia Roumeli, a few miles due south, to catch the last ferry east to Sfakia at four. Dinner at a taverna then back at the villa by eight. He had it all figured out.

They headed upwards through the trees. Dry leaves crackled underfoot; Graham held fir branches back to prevent them lashing into her face. Silke was glad of the mottled shade, the bird-calls, the herbal fragrance that permeated the air. God she loved days like these – outdoors, panoramic views of peaks opening up ahead, with Graham in his element, heading an expedition into terra incognita, unwittingly exuding a mild sense of danger but also that medical corps nous to overcome any disquiet about things going awry. And now there was the thrill of starting a family. Perhaps they might even make love on a mountain-side.

At the tree line, the air was cool, the sky a little overcast. A lunar landscape of limestone rocks and stones lay ahead, with the mist and snow of the mountains beyond. Silke's T-shirt was soaked, her eyes stinging again.

"Shit," Graham huffed, taking off the rucksack to sit down for a drink and study the map. "We should be heading downhill by now."

"The gorge," she panted. "Where is it?"

"Dunno. The map doesn't show any mountains. It must be on the other side of them."

He gauged the peaks ahead against the map as she slumped against a rock. Even when out of his comfort zone, he had a heroic quality about him: focused, unflustered, intent on getting them back on track.

"Here," he gestured, handing her the bottle. "But take it easy. Bread roll?"

She took the bottle and looked at the water. Barely a cup-ful left. Washing her eyes was out of the question. How stupid to have brought only half a litre, and used most of that already. She took a sip as he unearthed the rucksack's contents, searching for the rolls. Cosmetic bag. Newspaper. Banana. Muesli bar. After-sun. Passports. Plane tickets. The kagoul and jogging pants she'd forgotten to take out.

"Hurrah," he proclaimed, handing her a roll.

"So what now?" She questioned, expressionless, wiping the corners of her eyes.

"Well, if we're going to catch the ferry, we've got to go downhill – now. If we head south-westish, that should bring us to the gorge."

She searched his face, bothered by his sudden certainty – the same certainty that had once resulted in them crawling up Helvellyn in a force eight gale.

"And if we don't make it?"

"We'll stay in the port tonight."

"What about water? Should we go and get some snow?"

She already sensed his answer.

"We don't have time. Besides, we're bound to come to a stream at some point."

He stood up, planted a foot on a rock in the pose of a Victorian gentleman-explorer and swung the rucksack over his shoulder as she unwrapped her rations.

"Anyway," he shrugged, taking a bite of his roll, "we have to keep going."

He held out a hand to help her up. She took it, chewing with difficulty, her mouth already crying out with thirst.

They descended through the pathless wood in silence, angling across the steepening hillside. Her toes pressed against the boots she'd bought for the trip, her shins hurt from the constant braking. She identified the dry aroma of oregano growing among the dead grass, but was too hot and tired to look, eyes raging with lemon juice fire, hair an itching mass as if swarming with nits.

A mistake to have kept it so long, not to have tried a bob. How brave the girls back in London were with their cropped hair. Hair longer on one side than the other. Hair dyed white or pink. Hair artfully tousled for that sexypunky look. But that wasn't her, not now at least, on the wrong side of thirty. Or most other architects she knew. Besides, the kudos would last a day before the self-loathing set in. All made worse by Graham saying it suited her.

He spotted the line of a trail below, hugging the contour of the hillside. It had to be the path they'd missed. Uplifted, they took it. But in no time it dwindled out above a rock-face – only to start again at its base, some five metres below.

He clambered down the near-vertical face, feeling for ledges, then sprang off to jump the last two metres with a parachute landing fall. She threw the rucksack down then began the descent, trying to ignore the drop as he directed her foot placements and hand-holds, then jumped as he'd done, rolling over on hitting the ground. Silke stood up, astonished; she'd never done anything like that before.

They took the new trail down into a glade of rugged oaks and outcrops until it too disappeared, then continued west, a sharp slope below on their left. At a clearing, a distant ridge presented itself, pine trees speared the sky. It had to be the gorge.

She walked briskly, leaving Graham behind, then scrambled up the incline to face a huge void with some thin clouds of mist below. She was standing on the edge of a sheer drop. A dead sheep lay on the rocks some 200 metres below. She stepped back at once, hollow inside – one more step or a slip and she'd have fallen headlong to join it.

She retreated to the clearing and sat on a rock, staring at the grass thrusting up between the stones, head in her hands, as if about to be sick. There had been no sign, no warning.

"Hey, what's happening?" Graham grinned, trying to keep spirits up.

"I almost got killed, that's what," she snapped, struggling

to speak with such a dry mouth.

She outlined the void, the drop, the dead sheep.

"We're lost, Gray. Completely, utterly, fucking lost. We've barely got any water left, we haven't seen a stream all day. We've missed the ferry, and now we can't even make it to your damned port. We don't know if the ravine over there is the right one – and look, everywhere is too steep to climb down."

She gesticulated towards the opposite hillside bathed in a rich green-blue shade.

"But we have to keep moving," he urged, "manage our pace and energy. If we stop, we'll get stiff."

"Not as stiff as if we fall down one of those bloody ravines!"

She turned to him with a mixture of anger and disgust, her sense of adventure gone.

"You're not doing a triathlon now, Graham. This isn't some orienteering jaunt with your drinking mates. And anyway, what's the point of running around like headless chickens?"

He sat down by her side to rummage inside the rucksack then broke the muesli bar in two, handing her half. The chocolate chip bits had melted, making it go a little gooey but she didn't care, eating it in silence before sucking the wrapper and licking her fingers like a child.

"We have to go back," she determined. "It's our only chance."

"But Sil, it's at least six or seven miles away, we're knackered – "

"Look, I'm not carrying on in the blind hope that everything will be all right just around the next effing corner. Because it won't. Just go up there and take a look for yourself."

He frowned.

"But if we go back we may have to spend the night on the mountain."

She got to her feet and extended a hand to help him up.

"Well, we better get a move on then, hadn't we?"

Silke had never seen so many stars. The snowy mountain tops in the distance were jagged, rotten teeth, framed on either side by dark purple hills that dropped into the fjord-like chasm below. That oregano scent everywhere. A sheep-bell clinked across the valley. The sound might have offered hope that civilisation was nearby, if they had any idea where they were or which way to go. As it was, they had no compass. No proper map. No energy.

It did not feel cold. They'd stuffed dry leaves and newspaper pages into their shorts and T-shirts for the night, like vagrants. Silke also had the kagoul and jogging pants, but was still warm from the walk. The clear sky meant the temperature would soon plummet though. She closed her sore eyes, only for the precipice with the dead sheep to shriek back at her like the stairwell in *Vertigo*.

The day had been a disaster. She'd become a walking machine pounding across the arid terrain – over-heating, running on empty – with no interest in anything other than how to manage her yelling eyes and plant her swollen feet. She didn't know which was worse – the exhaustion, pain or dehydration. If they still had water, had stumbled across a stream, a pool, anything, it would have given them such a boost.

And what about tomorrow? Would – could – they make it back? The answer had to be *no*. The geology all around was limestone. Waterless, unrelenting. And they were too lost, too weak. As good as dead. The thought seemed far-fetched for an intelligent, educated woman like her. Yet it was true. Their corpses would be found in time, eyes pecked out, identifiable only from the passports that would have a use on this walk after all.

She'd never see her mother again. Her father. Her brother. Her dog Rollo. Everyone she knew. The little Grahams she'd so wanted. She envisaged her mother's worry at the unexplained absence, her stricken reaction to the news, her grief-laden journey from Copenhagen to this spot. She turned onto her side, and began crying into the hard ground.

Graham extended a hand across her forearm, and pulled her closer.

Graham. Medical researcher, ex-Army – man of action, survivor. Right to save the water, the banana, to use the newspaper for insulation. A man for a crisis, but he generated them too.

She felt he was to die for when they'd met, with his English humour and Alain Delon looks, but a fat lot of good either had been on this abject frog-march. And good breeding stock or not, if he loved her, then why hadn't he taken more care of her?

It started to get light around four. By five the sun streamed through the trees, lighting on the pine needles and cones around them. Neither had slept much on the hard, cold ground, and both now gawped sullen-eyed at the vapours rising from the glacier of mist covering the gorge below.

Graham got up with difficulty, limped to a tree and slid his back down its trunk to sit right knee jacked up, arm outstretched. Silke slunk down beside him, solid-stiff, weak and sunburnt, mouth hangover-dry. They sat in silence for some time as if waiting for their blood-flow to start like lizards in the morning sun.

"What about our pee?" she croaked. "Should we drink it?"

"No," he answered at length. "It'd only speed up the dehydration. Like drinking sea-water. The body can last four days without water. We just have to get going."

Four days. That was all that remained of her life. Unbelievable. She pictured the snow the day before. What fools they'd been not to get some. They could have had a feeding frenzy, filled the bottle. Instead, she didn't even have any spit to swallow.

Their only hope was rain – a sudden monsoon – to stand under the trees, mouths agape like baby birds, capturing every drop. But the sky was cloudless. In an hour or so the day would be an open oven.

They finished the last of the water and banana, then set off into the centre of the sun. Silke staggered forward, as if walking in a suit of armour, but it was too much. Her feet were blistered, shins sore, unable to bear any weight. Worse still, she now had no impetus. And this, after hoping a fresh start would be invigorating.

"I can't," she wept, sinking to the ground, alarmed that her lack of energy was so debilitating. "I'm just shattered."

Graham knelt to massage her aching calves. She tried again, but to no effect.

"Try crawling," he suggested. "We can't just stay here."

After twenty metres on her hands and knees, he took her through some stretching exercises. She tried walking again, using him as a crutch. Slowly the stiffness began to ease, but everywhere looked the same. Hard. Featureless. Oppressive.

What an idiot she felt for not checking the map at the start, to have placed her life in his hands. If she made it out alive, never again would she rely on anyone so completely.

They'd only gone another hundred metres or so when Graham spotted the rock-face from the day before. It seemed like fantastic news, presenting a way back, a way out. But they could barely walk, let alone climb.

He stood at its base, scrutinising the cracks and fissures, then delineated a route to scale it. She stared at the silent behemoth. One false move would result in a broken skull or limb, halting them forever.

"I can't," she wailed, apathetic to how pathetic she sounded. "I just don't have any strength."

He looked for another way up, but on either side the rock deepened into tall cliff-faces.

"Just try," he coaxed. "We've no choice. I'll go first. Watch where I put my hands and feet. Then I'll guide you through it. And pull you up over the last stretch."

The plan sounded so simple, logical. But what if she fell? What would he do – make the precarious descent and stay with her, or carry on to save his own skin?

As he neared the top, a loosened boulder flashed past, grazing her arm. Now it was her turn.

"Keep your body against the face," he coached from above. "And don't look down. Make sure your hand and foot-holds are secure before you push off. And don't rush."

She had to concentrate like never before. Use the very last of her energy reserves. She placed her right foot on the half-ledge as he'd done and felt for his first hand-hold, brushing away some loose pebbles. Then pulled herself up by the fingertips, in slow motion it seemed, and planted her left foot on the same ledge. She was now completely off the ground, trembling a little, frisked against the scarred rock-face.

"That's it," he coached again, "you're doing great!"

Maintaining the pressure in her fingertips on the narrow

ledges, she repeated the sequence, gaining another half metre. Then another, and another, until she could feel a strong grasp on her left forearm. He hauled her onto the small plateau where they lay panting, as if after sex. She then rolled towards the shade of a tree, and closed her eyes to the moistureless air.

There was no sign of him when she came to, head throbbing, only the distant sound of voices before some footsteps quickened across the brush. A dark, middle-aged man with a craggy face and thick black moustache knelt by her side, glimmering in and out of focus. He held a water pouch to her lips.

"Nero," he insisted in a husky voice. "Mikros."

She raised her head, making out a leather game bag strapped across his camouflage jacket and a rifle in the nondescript grass.

"Little," Graham instructed, somewhere nearby. "I think he means drink *a little* at a time."

She let the water trickle into her mouth and swallowed, painfully at first, then took some more.

"Than you," she murmured, breathing in the stranger's tobacco breath.

Graham helped her up as the hunter waved both hands several times to the east.

"Zkromos," he stressed, "zkromos."

"Efharisto," Graham acknowledged, supporting Silke from the side. "He must mean that's the way back."

The man helped Silke to more water. She took a mouthful, then another, until it dribbled down her chin. Already her body was recharging, like a garden surging back to life. She guzzled some more then closed her eyes, picturing the clear stream in the photograph from the day before.

My Brothers Would Kill You

He'd never known such pain. His chest, right ear and foot throbbed; even breathing hurt. And that pounding behind his right eye – as if he were no longer a young man with a damaged eyeball but a damaged eyeball attached to a young man. All he could do was inhale the smell of disinfectant and lie still – bandages binding him from head to foot, arms strapped across his chest like a dead pharaoh.

Sunlight slanted through a window to his left, giving the ward the warmth of a greenhouse. It must be late morning. He could remember the night before in waves – the iodine in A&E, being carried into the ward as two old men coughed and groaned, unattended. There was no sign of them now, their beds already stripped and made, flowers and photographs long since cleared away.

A clack of heels echoed down the corridor then stopped, leaving a small woman in glasses and a white coat by the side of his bed. She inspected a tube from his chest to some liquid below which babbled occasionally when he exhaled.

"You can see?" She inquired, her accent converting the *s* into a heavy *sh*, as she wagged her stethoscope prongs towards a large damp patch shaped like South America on the flaking, white-washed wall opposite.

He tried to focus his working eye on the continental water stain, then looked to the window where a distant cloud had cauliflowered into the blue.

"It is," she began, then left the utterance hanging in midair. "I not know words… Everyone says that and this, but nobody does nothing… How we say in Greece, kaos. Like last night for you, I think?"

"Oh."

He recalled the baseball bats raining down, the jump over the wall into the darkness below. But not how he'd got to the hospital or any procedure to insert a tube into his chest.

"Pardon," she smiled, sitting on the edge of the bed. "I am Dr Mariapolous. How you feel?"

"Terrible," he struggled. "I'm in agony, all over. There's this incredible pressure in – "

"Sorry," she interrupted, raising the palm of her hand. "Slow please. My English is a little."

The hand turned into a gesture of a gap between finger and thumb, then plopped two tablets into the glass of water on his bedside unit. He spelt out the words as the mixture frothed into a chalky grey then started to clear.

"Here," she beckoned, extending the glass to his mouth. "For pain."

He craned forward and drank. Some of the solution dribbled onto his chest, seeping into the bandages.

"Me eye," he moaned. "Will I see again?"

She took a pencil torch from her top pocket and clicked it on. Phil could feel the heat from the light roving over his jammed eye, but saw nothing.

"I think so," she considered before clicking her tongue while breaking the neck of an invisible bird. "But bone is broken."

She donned her stethoscope, placed the teat on his chest and ordered him to inhale. She tapped his chest with two joined fingers, listening with the intensity of a safe-breaker. She nodded again then summarised the extent of his injuries while pointing to parts of her body, wringing more birds' necks and holding up different numbers of fingers as if playing charades. Seven broken ribs. Four broken fingers. Two broken teeth. Broken eye socket. Broken ankle. Ruptured ear drum. Stab wound. Punctured lung. Loss of blood. A lot of blood.

It was meant to be a lads' holiday on Simnos. Sun, sex and sangria. A way of flicking two fingers up at Kirsty after the split. But late on the first night the three amigos were slogging back alone to the resort when ten or more mopeds carrying passengers flew past – so close the lads had to back up against the loose dry-stone wall above the sea. Phil was struck by something heavy across the shoulders, knocking him to the ground.

He got up, helped by Snowy. A group of men stood around them, some with baseball bats, acrid smoke billowing from the revving engines. Phil tried to figure out what was happening – they'd done nothing wrong. A man with a ram's nose yabbered at John, then headbutted him. John lashed out with a fist. The others started punching and kicking Phil and Snowy.

"Leg it!" John yelled, breaking free to sprint downhill.

Snowy jumped over the retaining wall to flee uphill into the woods. Phil turned to run up the road – to be faced by about fifteen men, encircling him, two or three deep. He held out his hands and felt a hot pain below his left ribs, like a deep wasp sting. He sank to the ground, clutching his side with his right hand, then curled up on the road, only for bats to start pummelling him with the mechanical regularity of a chain gang. Each blow was powerful, and meant. He'd been in fights before, back in Leeds, and could look after himself, but this was too much. He wasn't going to survive.

He scrambled to shoulder-charge the nearest attacker then dived over the seaward wall into the pitch-black below. A heart-stopping silence.

He crashed into a branch then through some more before landing on his right-hand side, winded and dazed, the taste of blood in his mouth. He tried to take stock, surprised not to be in greater pain, then began folding part of his ripped shirt to press it against the stab wound.

Above, voices. Mopeds buzzed downhill. A lightbeam searched between the firs to his left, picking out rocks – he could feel its warmth beside him. He had to move, but his right foot was immobilised, as if caught in a trap. He dragged himself forward, crawling through tall, wet grass with a strong herbal smell.

Below, mopeds began careering across the beach as if a group of giddy teenagers were carving figures of eight in the sand for fun. But this was no game – their headlights were criss-crossing the hillside, searching for him. One warmed his back. He fell to his belly at once. Other spot-lights then congregated on the area where he lay, briefly touching the mouth of a concrete tunnel ahead. Eventually they moved away.

He hauled himself towards the tunnel and groped his way inside. It had a sour, salty smell, like a broken drain. It had to be a stormwater outlet above the beach. But it provided cover. Safety. Respite.

By early afternoon the ward was hot and airless, despite the open windows. The painkillers had done little to stop his eye and foot transmitting incessant signals. He lay squelch-ing in sweat, thirsty but unable to reach the water on the bedside unit, bandages soaked from lunch – a greasy soup he'd had to balance on his sternum then flick towards his mouth with a teaspoon. He was dependent on the nurses' infrequent rounds for food, water and bed-pan. But none of them spoke English or seemed to care.

Maybe it was retribution for the furore the night before, when he'd found himself lying on a table, a bright bulb swaying overhead, as an elderly woman in a white uniform handed John a roll of toilet paper with an order to mop up the blood.

"Jasus," John had remonstrated, "he doesn't need cleanin, he needs to stop feckin bleedin! For Chrys' sake, will you just go an fetch the doctor!"

She'd shouted back in Greek, hands waving. An unshaven doctor strolled in, chewing gum and smoking a cigarette which never left his mouth. He wore an opened white coat, jeans and a crumpled grey T-shirt with sweat stains. He talked briefly to her, cigarette wagging, then took some surgical scissors and a dark brown bottle from a glass cabinet. Without a word he cut into Phil's T-shirt to reveal a chest that looked as though it had been rubbed down with sandpaper, then unscrewed the lid of the bottle and emptied it over him at arm's length. The electric shock of pain made Phil scream. Unmoved, the doctor glared at John as if to say this was all his fault.

Outside, the sun seemed to be intensifying. A fragrance like freshly cut flowers wafted into the ward. At least his sense of smell was still intact. But how long would it take to recover? How long would he be stuck here?

To think, only twenty-four hours ago he'd been tucking into the in-flight drinks trolley. Had watched Snowy get nowhere with the stewardess. Snickered at John's jokes. Led the team talk about sharking tactics and the points system for the week ahead. Declared at customs he was available to the women of Simnos. And had later chatted up those girls at the taverna – each one in a mini-skirt, heels and make-up, looking stunning. They were cousins from Piraeus on a hen weekend, mostly married – up for flirting and tequila slammers, but also looking out for each other like a family of meerkats. There was no chance of going missing in action with any of them, so the lads had decided to go clubbing.

"How would your family react if you brought me home?" he'd asked the unattached one before they left.

"My mother would love you," she'd glowered without hesitation. "But my father would hate you. And my brothers would kill you."

In the corridor, a nurse was talking to someone. John or Snowy perhaps, come to visit him at last. Two swarthy men in pressed white shirts entered, one short with a thick moustache, the other huge and sporting a suit jacket around his shoulders like a seventies' filmstar. They pulled up chairs to sit side by side on his right. Phil looked down, disconcerted by the slop stains, the reek of his stormdrain-infused BO.

"You seem to have been," the smaller one smiled, "in the wars?"

"You can say that again," Phil huffed, relieved at the standard of English, the chance to find out what was going on.

He tried to sit upright, but pain screamed through his chest.

"Please," the man interjected, raising a hand as if signalling traffic to stop. "No need."

A delayed wave of pain boomed down Phil's right-hand side.

"We are police," the stranger carried on. "The hospital has asked us to consider the cause of your injuries. Tell us what happened."

About time. Phil started running through the incident, eager to relay the sequence of events. They nodded at intervals.

"And where is your passport?" The man cut in after the second wave of mopeds. "We must see it."

Phil looked puzzled. What did that have to do with anything?

The man repeated the question slowly as if he hadn't understood.

"I'm not sure," Phil ruminated briefly, keen to return to his account.

The inquisitor's mouth narrowed, the pleasant disposition drained from his face.

"And where are your friends?" He burned, as if insulted.

"I dunno."

He stood up, then pointed from hip-height.

"I said," he strained, teeth bared, "where are your friends?"

Heat shot to Phil's face. His breathing shortened. He recalled from biology at school that a rat is harmless when going about its business but becomes hunched and aggressive when cornered.

The man turned to pace the ward, hands on hips, shaking his head.

"I'm sorry for my colleague," the bigger one interposed with a smile, slipping a hand into his jacket. "He just wants to be sure your friends are OK."

He produced a badge and held it towards Phil.

"My ID," he indicated then put it back and slipped off his jacket.

But Phil hadn't asked for his ID. Nor had they been taking notes. And he hadn't even got to the beating yet.

"We need to take care of your passport," the big man proceded in a brisk tone, arranging the jacket on the back of his chair. "Where is it?"

Phil checked himself, unsettled. It was back at the apartment, at the bottom of his unpacked suitcase.

"I'm not sure," he lied as best he could.

The man's face dropped. He stood up, bent over Phil and grabbed the greasy bandages below his neck, twisting them tight, pulling him to his face. Phil whimpered as pain turned to agony.

"Get off!" he blurted, trying to wriggle out of his straight-jacket, "get off me!"

The man threw Phil back into the pillows – then leant forward to land a bone-crunching punch in his face. Phil cried out, blood splashing from the bridge of his nose into his eyes. The first man advanced to hold him down from the other side, shouting for his passport. The big one struck again.

"Get out!" a woman's voice shrieked, piercing the fray. "Get out of my hospital!"

Phil squinted through blood-stinging eyes. It was the doctor. The first man let go.

"How dare you come here," she raged, then stepped towards the tall one and reached up to slap him across the face.

Phil looked on in disbelief. What was she doing, hitting a policeman? Let alone this Goliath?

"Go!" she shouted, stamping her foot, pointing the way outside.

She turned on the first man and started boxing him about the ears. He ducked, raising both hands to parry her blows. The men backed towards the door as she stood her ground at the end of the bed like a mountain goat. The first man slid out, but the big one turned to point at Phil.

"We will be waiting for you," he warned, then left.

The doctor turned to sit on the bed, breathing loudly through her nose. She plinked two tablets in a glass of water, then took some cotton wool from the bedside unit and started to wipe blood from his face.

"They were police," he exclaimed, stupefied.

She raised her head and dabbed away, leaning forward in deep concentration to inspect his nose as the glass of water fizzed.

"Shhh," she calmed, almost as an afterthought. "You have broken nose."

Her touch was so gentle and precise – hard to equate with the she-wolf that had just seen off the aggressors.

"These are not police," she spat in a hushed tone, raising the cleared solution to his lips. "You must trust no one in this country. And not leave my hospital until I say."

Phil sank back into his pillows, able to see his scoured and bruised body now the bandages had loosened. He'd assumed the attack the night before had been a case of thugs being thugs, but clearly now it was part of something bigger, more sinister. He was being targeted.

Maybe it was linked to the fracas with some local lads in the first club after a round of speed-drinking had fuelled John's courage to dance with a bored-looking girl who turned out to be the barman's fiancée. Or to his passport – to sell on the black market. But why his? Why not just break into any apartment and steal one?

He didn't have a clue. All he knew was that he had to get out. But couldn't move. Had nowhere to go. Had no one to trust except the doctor. But even she knew more than she was letting on. Worse still, the men had tracked him down, and were probably still there, somewhere, waiting.

He shut his left eye, trying to think of a worse time in his life. There wasn't one. He'd thought earlier he might die here from natural causes, but now there was a press gang waiting to finish him off. If his wounds didn't get him, the cut-throats would. This was where he was going to die.

But he wasn't ready for death. He needed to see Mum and Dad, to say goodbye, to tell them he loved them. Right now they'd be doing the shopping or getting lunch ready, joking about how he'd be trying to swim off a hangover – with Becky in her room, singing into the microphone of a brush while joining the dance routine of a girl-band on full blast.

And another thing… Where were the lads? Why hadn't they visited – as he'd have done if the boot had been on the other foot? He pictured them sunbathing and chatting up girls on the beach. Some mates they were. Or maybe they'd had it worse – been rounded up and slaughtered like sheep?

No. The imposters had pressed for their whereabouts. So they had to be alive. In fact, this was the only positive from the encounter. But if they did visit, they'd be taken apart. He had to warn them to stay away. But how? And what if the nurses were in league with the duo? Better maybe to look after himself, in case the men returned. To smother him with a pillow. Smash his skull in with baseball bats.

He began to mumble the Lord's Prayer, surprised he could remember the words.

Dusk was deepening when he woke, stiff and sore, pain driving a spike through his forehead. A young woman was sitting at the end of the bed, almost a silhouette though he could make out a suit, long brown hair, pretty nose. He wanted to disown his dishevelled state and rotten stench, the drool hanging from his chin.

"Are you OK?" she soothed in a Home Counties accent, leaning forward to pat his hand.

Somehow Phil knew he could trust her.

"Well, I've been better," he slurred in a sotto voice. "An looked better an all."

She gave a faint smile and stroked his hand.

"My name is Alison. I'm from the British Embassy. I'm here to help. We know what's happened to you. We have to get you out of here."

Oh, thank you God. He was going to live.

"Can you walk?" She murmured.

"I don't think so."

"Well," she tried, with a kind face, "let's have a go and get you to your feet, shall we?"

She helped manoeuvre his legs then clasped his torso and eased him to the edge of the bed. He could see his right foot for the first time now – it had gone mauve and ballooned horribly, too swollen to be put in a cast. She picked up the glass jar of the burbling chest-drain, and lugged him to his feet, letting him use her as a crutch. The muscles and tendons in his legs screeched at having to bear the dead-weight of his body. The pair inched towards the window like stragglers in a three-legged race, each step harder than the last, pausing whenever he yelped.

Eventually, he looked outside from the fifth floor of the L-shaped building, a landscaped area of cypress trees below, a sparse constellation of yellow streetlights beyond. She gestured towards a black BMW by the entrance.

"See that parked car down there?" She asked, drawing her head back. "There are two men in it, waiting for you. They're probably working in shifts with another pair. Somehow we need to get you out of here without them seeing us."

He edged his head forward briefly then drew it back as she'd done. She guided him back to bed. Every step sent razor blades down his legs. The pressure above his right eye was unbearable.

"I'm in agony," he grimaced, once back in bed.

She perched on the left side of his bed and helped him to a glass of water. But what he needed was some painkillers.

"Can you tell us what's goin on?" He winced.

She folded her arms and looked down, mulling it over.

"All in good time," she answered at length. "Do you think you can make it to the lift?"

He remembered it from the night before. It was some distance away.

"I can try."

"Good," she replied, patting his hand again. "I'll come and get you at midnight. But you must be ready. And don't tell a soul you're leaving."

He frowned.

"But what about me mates? Where are they?"

"Don't worry," she reassured, squeezing his hand. "We've got your friends. They're safe."

She moved off the bed and stood up.

"So who are those guys?" He questioned, shifting uncomfortably. "Why are they waiting for me?"

She faced the window in thought, sighed then sat down again.

"You'll have heard of the mafia in Italy," she started. "Well, there is one in Greece too."

She explained that two nights ago a mobster's daughter had been raped by an English-speaking tourist outside a club. They thought Phil was that rapist. Once the police had established the crime had been committed before the lads' arrival, they took John and Snowy into protective custody then called the Embassy. The intruders wanted Phil's passport to prevent him from leaving the island.

Mafia. Rape. Passport. The words exploded in his head. And explained everything. What idiots they'd been to go up against those lads in the club, inadvertently marking themselves out as targets. He felt sick. But knew now he had to walk, however bad the pain.

"Out here, it's an eye for an eye," she shrugged, then rested her hand on his. "Blood must have blood. Facts don't enter the equation. It's a question of honour, you see. A vendetta."

He remained staring at the ceiling after she'd gone, still taking it in. Mistaken identity. An indiscriminate attack the night before, like wasps stinging the nearest passer-by, regardless of whether they'd disturbed the nest or not. And now a premeditated assault. If anyone touched Becky he'd probably feel much the same, but would at least know he was taking on the right man. Now he was being hunted down by a death squad for something he hadn't done. Worse still, they knew where he was, trussed up, unable to move.

His breathing quickened. His sweat filled the stifling air. It was a good job he hadn't taken any painkillers since waking. He needed to listen to every click or clack down the corridor – every fly buzzing in and out the window – just to keep himself awake – alive – in case they returned to finish him off.

Thank God for Alison. He needed her so much. But what if she didn't come back?

Time dragged. When the lights came on at last, the doctor stood by the door, her hair in a bun. She wheeled in a metal trolley rattling with bottles and instruments, stating that his chest-drain had to be removed. She set to work in silence, her face a study in concentration and concern that made him regret his earlier doubts. He wanted to explain the situation, thank her, say goodbye. But couldn't risk it.

In no time she was gone, leaving a book-sized bandage over his chest. Silence. He wondered if the hospital was open all hours, like back home. Did it have guards? And if so, what chance would they stand against the opposition? The two men were probably just waiting for the day staff to leave before entering, unnoticed and unchallenged, to slit his throat like a pig's.

He had to be ready to help Alison help him, walk on hot coals if necessary. Mind over matter. He lifted himself to his feet, the searing pain ten times worse when upright, and tried some football warm-ups in slow-motion. Impossible. He reached out for the next bed and clung onto it, moving one excruciating step at a time towards the window, then peered below, keeping within the shadow of the curtain.

The stake-out car was still there.

"Are you ready?" Alison whispered, her hand on his.

He opened his left eye. She was wearing glasses, her hair in a bun too.

"Yep, I'm ready."

He used her to heave himself to his feet, then hobbled to the door and down the dimly-lit corridor. The hospital was silent, still. It seemed like they were the only ones there.

She steered him through a door marked with two red signs – one an X across a stick-man, the other a porter's trolley – into an area stacked with large laundry baskets. She pressed a button by a steel lift door. There was a clunk, a gear-changing scrunch, then a gradual hum, low-level and deafening at the same time.

He bit his bottom lip, on full alert. He was breathing hard, heart skipping in irregular beats. All evening he'd wanted nothing more than to escape, but now he'd left the ward he missed the scant security it offered. He was adrift on an open sea of risk. They would surely be seen. Then what?

The door slid open. She hauled him inside then yanked the inner black concertina door closed and pressed a button on the control panel. The outer doors of the lift clacked shut, leaving only a square of light from their small head-height window, casting one side of her face in shadow.

The service lift moved off, light receding until they were submerged in darkness. Light from the floor below burst into the enclosed space then disappeared again as they descended further.

Phil's mouth had gone dry. He searched Alison's face for some reassurance. She was looking down, eyes hard to read behind the glasses – half her face the dark side of the moon, then fully gone. A world away from the cheerful guardian from earlier.

But of course. She was in league with them. He tensed. Light flooded in. She'd told him to keep quiet to avoid detection. What a fool he'd been. The touching said it all – no diplomat would do that. *Trust no one in this country.* Darkness rose as he saw the welcoming party ahead. The two men. The moped gang. Ready to tape over his mouth, bundle him into the boot of the BMW. Then drive to a secluded wood, put a bullet in his brain and bury him in a shallow grave.

Light streamed in again. He lunged forward to bang his palm against the black mesh of the concertina door.

"What are you doing?" She exclaimed, blocking him as the light withdrew.

"I wanna go back!" he cried out in the sudden dark, tears welling from nowhere.

She grabbed his arm to prevent him from reaching the control panel.

"Get off me!" he shouted, grappling with her, shards of pain stabbing his chest.

The lift filled with light again, then bumped to a halt. She let go. He looked in horror at the door. It started to slide open. A well-lit service area with a dark basement car park beyond. Concrete pillars. Markings on the tarmac. A small blue Fiat.

He stayed put, panting, eyes flitting from pillar to pillar. She shook her head, brushed a hand over her jacket arms, then tugged the inner door open. A white-coated figure stepped into view. It was the doctor. She studied his wild look then moved forward to take his arm.

He looked at her in disbelief. What on earth was she doing here?

"Shhh," she hushed, ushering him towards the car. "This way."

She took off her white coat and gave it to Alison, who scrambled it on. He shut his eyes and hung his head, shaking it slowly, fighting back a fresh surge of tears. He had been so wrong. And these women were being so brave – for him. He raised his left hand to shield his face as it began to contort, and sank back against a pillar, unable to stop crying.

"Go," the doctor ordered softly. "You must go."

She took his left arm and Alison the right. Together they guided him towards the car.

Yellow light flipped across the dashboard as he lay hunched on the back seat in great discomfort.

"Keep your head down," Alison directed. "We're going to have to pass them."

An indicator ticked as they began a right turn, bumping over something. He recoiled in acute pain.

"They're just ahead," she clipped, the words barely audible. "I can't talk now."

He could picture the two men in the BMW. Watching. Smoking. Waiting.

"It's OK," she confirmed at last. "We've passed them. I'm

taking you to your friends. They've got your things. Then onto a private airfield, where a plane will take you all to Athens. From there you can fly to England."

It was over. Finally over. They'd made it. He levered himself onto an elbow to look back at the hospital towering over the parked cars, and noticed the flash of a brake-light – like a night-sight on infrared with someone about to pull the trigger.

Exposure

The last subject left an hour ago and I'm just about to lock up the studio for the night. The day's gone OK, the afternoon easier than the morning, more profitable too. But then the fashion work always is. I call it *fashion* to attract the girls – make them feel good about themselves, that they're in safe hands and on the right track with their career. But really it's mutton dressed as lamb.

It's hardly what I set out to do, but it pays the bills. I wanted to be a landscape painter, but could never master clouds at art school and found photography a cinch: as long as you get the light right and know what you're doing in the dark room, you can't go wrong. Besides, who wants landscape paintings nowadays?

People are unsure when I tell them what I do. They get the portrait side of things – families, couples, pets – that I don't do much outdoor work, and specialise in catalogue stuff for underwear firms. But it doesn't take long for the jokes to start. "A shit or bust business, I suppose," they'll say, or "Well, I'm pleased you've got that off your chest." One mate I go round to have dinner with even does roast chicken every time, just so he can ask, "So Harry, what'll you have – breast or breast?"

It's more technical than they think. Fixed tripod or hand-held, colour or black and white, light source, shutter speed, composition, close-ups, digital remastering and so on. But what really makes or breaks an image is knowing how much light the skin can take, what colours to use for clothing, background, make-up.

Especially make-up. When a shoot is booked, we send the girls our Ts & Cs with a contract to sign and return. The covering letter asks them not to wear make-up, but they always do. So the first half an hour is usually spent taking it off, which makes them all upset.

I understand if it's their first time, and don't mind that much since I charge by the hour. But if they've signed up for the Platinum service and I've got the make-up artist in, it's my clock that's ticking. And when it's a girl with no money from somewhere up north you wish for their sake they didn't have shit for brains. But all they can see is their big dream, to become the next Cheryl Cole or whoever.

They usually come with their mum. They love their mum and their mum loves them. They think of her as their best friend. True, the mums are supportive, protective. Anxious too. But sometimes they're fooling themselves, and you wonder where it's leading; shouldn't they be encouraging Sharon or Bev to get a proper job like the rest of us? And some can be pushy, with their own agenda, asking what to do next, how to get a break, can I have a word with this magazine or that. I'm not an agent for Christ's sake.

I let the old biddies in for the first five minutes of a shoot, when the girl still has all her clothes on and I'm taking blanks mostly while coming out with some chat to settle her. "So where are you from then?" "What are you looking to do?" "Do you like animals?" "Tell me about your boyfriend." That kind of thing.

They'll have been a teen queen and the school hottie, you see, used to getting their own way. But once they're in the studio, they're a fish out of water, nervous as hell, still trying to do the pouts and poses they've been practising in front of the bedroom mirror all year. And what I tell them to do goes in one ear and out the other at first.

So the chat is critical. It helps build up their confidence; the mums' too. I usually wear a wedding ring and slip in that my wife'll be along later or that I had a nightmare weekend as coach to my son's under-9s side. The mums like that. A single guy would be a lone wolf. A shark. A predator.

After the initial shoot I take a break before the main one. I have a think about all sorts. Light levels mostly. Skin tones of course. Which colours would suit them. Do they have a natural smile or not. What angles would work best. Looking up or down. What's needed for setting up. It also gives them a chance to see mum alone, discuss their big day so far and hopefully agree I seem "nice" or whatever.

But then the mother has to wait with Janice on reception. No girl is going to undress and feel sexy with her mum hovering in the wings, and it doesn't allow me to focus either.

This is where it counts, and the girls know it. I start with the clothes on. Then blouse undone. Then just the bra. Then topless. By now they're more or less used to the camera, studio and me – and feel it's OK to unbutton their top and take off their bra because I'm a pro and have seen it all before.

I usually get all the shots they need in the first ten minutes or so, with the missy standing, front-on. But I spin the session out to take it into a second hour by getting her to do different poses. Looking up. Looking down. Looking over the shoulder. Looking happy. Looking sad. And all over again with her sitting down.

"Once more," I'll say, "but with feeling. That's it. Hold it. Perfect."

They're up for it now, confident as hell. They believe this is acting, that they're the new Kate Beckinsale – and today is the first day of the rest of their lives. But really they're just sitting there doing whatever I tell them. "Crawl across the floor," I could say, and they'd be off like a shot. As much sense and initiative as Dumbo the elephant.

Once the session's over, I'm straight into post-production, sifting through the images on-screen. I like to start when they're still getting changed, just in case the resolution means their skin has come out in corned beef blotches and I need to take a few more shots. But to be honest, that rarely happens. And there's not much a bit of air-brushing can't put right nowadays.

Do I fancy them? They're good-looking, most of them, sure. But they're also too young, all skin and bone, or already have Botox lips and over-sized implants that are only ever going to get them a job in porn. And you lose your appetite somehow when it's handed to you on a plate. Besides, I'm no spring chicken these days. And more to the point, I've got a business to run – work to win, contracts to manage. Reputation is everything in this line of work.

Not that I don't have a laugh. Sometimes Janice will have a lark on the computer, sticking the faces of the ones with bossy mothers onto different boobs, under the title *A Right Pair*.

That's about it really. Janice sends on the photos a week later for them to tout to the modelling agencies, tabloids, gents' magazines, poster printing firms, whoever. She could do it sooner but I like to be 100% sure the money has gone through first. You never know.

Do they find success? I've no idea. I never see them again.

The Evil One

Boo sat huddled by a radiator in the refectory, clasping a mug of tea in both hands, as I stroked her leg through her worsted skirt and watched the snow falling outside. She was tall and well-spoken with long mousey hair that fell onto her shoulders like a sixties model. It was hard to believe we were an item, especially since I was doing Theology, the uncoolest subject in the universe.

An ice-cold hand pressed against my neck.

"Willy," came Filth's faint London twang from behind.

I looked round, and there he was, smallish but stocky, blonde hair and green eyes, a cross between Robert Redford and Kirk Douglas.

"You pillock," I started.

"Hello, you must be Boo," he smoothed with teeth made for a toothpaste ad. "I'm Steven. Will's told me a lot about you. When he's not praying, of course."

Bastard. Comments like that could make her realise my prospects were limited to becoming a vicar.

"Well, my real name's Linda," she blushed. "But it looks like I must get used to Boo."

"Just as we must all get used to Will. As I'm sure we will one day."

He gave a look of mock-horror. She giggled, eyes locked onto him.

"All right, all right," I broke in. "Are you going to stand there or get Boo another tea?"

"Of course. What would you like, Linda? Tea? Coffee? Something stronger?"

"Tea please. That'd be lovely."

"Sorry," he smirked, "I meant something stronger than Will."

He burst out laughing, and so did she. Some friend, ridiculing me in front of my dream girl, flirting with her too. Bastard.

I'd only been able to get into university at Hull to study Art History and Theology. I'd planned to drop Theology on arrival, but soon learnt Art History had to be studied with another subject and I didn't have the grades to do anything else.

It wasn't all bad. I loved Boo and mucked about with Filth, whom I'd met at a party during freshers' week. As a drunken girl annoyed everyone there by taking flash photos, we talked about cricket, Bowie and girls. I'd only done it once – with a German nurse on a train that summer – but he was more experienced, so worth probing for tips.

Over those first few weeks we explored the area in his VW Beetle. Pubs. Clubs. The docks. He was good company, but there was always an edge.

"Banks, you slag," he would hiss, imitating Ray Winstone in the film *Scum*, "I'm the daddy around here, and don't you forget it."

By the time he returned, Boo had left and an idea to get even was slithering into my mind.

"You should see her housemate Tina," I broached, taking the mug from him. "Dark hair, blue eyes. Nice."

He sat down then leant forward.

"Is she the girl that was here earlier?" He pressed. "The one in the leopard-skin tights?"

I plinked a sugar cube into my tea, and concentrated on stirring it.

"Do you know," I reflected, glowing inside, "I think Tina does have a pair of tights like that…"

"So?" He pushed, eyes flitting from one scenario to another. "How can we meet?"

I blew the steam from my mug before taking a sip.

"Willy, can you fix something up?"

"Well, I'll see. I'm at Boo's tonight, so could try and have a word with Tina. How about lunch tomorrow?"

"Perfect," he drawled, slouching back. "But it must look natural."

The next day I sat waiting with him in the refectory.

"I don't do blind dates, darling," Tina had shone the night before, making Boo giggle. "I only do blind lust."

Filth looked around without a shred of nerves, then related how one of the first teamers had been beaten up by townies the night before. It was no surprise: the locals despised students, who hardly endeared themselves by mimicking the way Kingstonians said *err nerr*.

At ten past twelve, Boo was at the table with his hot date.

"What a palaver," Tina complained, banging her tray down. "Those cashiers are always over-charging."

His face dropped at her cropped hair, nose studs and *FUCK YOU* T-shirt.

"Tina, Filth," I introduced them.

"Well, hello," she smooched, squeezing onto a chair. "I can't wait to hear why you're called Filth."

He nodded, taking it in.

"Though I was expecting someone… Bigger?"

He swallowed, sunken by the laughter breaking out around him.

"Right, then," I gloated. "Better leave you two love-birds to it. See you later."

I left with Boo, flicking a V-sign at him from behind Tina then feigning a laugh as he looked on, eyes seething.

At around five I headed back to the refectory, noticing the word *SEXUAL* emblazoned on an A4-sized poster taped to the inside glass of the swing door. It contained a blurry, crudely cut-out photograph of someone with so much hair hacked away that his head looked too small for his body. Poor bloke, obviously the victim of a prank.

Hold on a minute. That figure looked familiar. I skim-read the text.

LOOKING FOR
SEXUAL
GRATIFICATION?

See
WILL KEMP
UNHUNKY STALLION

This macho stud could be yours!
Sincerity & subtlety kept to a minimum.
Hundreds of customers can't be wrong.
"The master is certainly full of spunk." (Julian)
"Das is gut! Ja." (Girl on a train)

SEE HIM IN ACTION
AT A HALL OF RESIDENCE NEAR YOU

Bastard.

This was Filth's handiwork all right. And me at my most naïve – I hadn't reckoned on reprisals at all.

Das is gut. Bastard – that fling was a secret. Stupid bastard too – the German was *ist*, not *is*. And the photo – taken by that drunken girl – not my best side at all, in fact I looked like a hunchback. Hundreds would have traipsed past the poster, including Boo. What would she make of it? And were there any more?

I looked back at the main concourse. A flimsy Will Kemp poster fluttered from every door and window.

I caught up with him in the bar, still panting from tearing down every copy in sight.

"You piece of shite," I began. "Just soooo evil."

"Willy," Filth crowed, top dog again, extending a hand. "Quits?"

Fair enough. We played back our recent duel, and I discovered he'd planned to apply weed-killer to the hillocks by the sports pitches so the dead grass would read: WILLY IS A WANKER. He'd even typed a letter from me to the Vice-Chancellor requesting to study Theology only.

I had to hand it to him – he was a class act. And I'd got off pretty lightly.

Two hours later we staggered out under a poacher's moon.

In the distance, seven figures were kicking in a snowman near the girls' accommodation block. We stood out against the snow as clearly as them. They exchanged words and bent down to scrape up some snow, then began to move forward as one, spreading out like encircling wolves.

"Just carry straight on," he steered, picking up speed. "Trust me."

If we carried on into their centre we'd be pulverised in a crossfire. But Filth's block was dead left.

Without warning, he sprinted off to it. In a second I was with him.

"Fuckin students!" one of them yelled in a Hull accent.

There was an eerie silence before a volley of snowballs slapped into the wall on our left. Something exploded in my right ear like a punch. I'd taken a direct hit from an iceball.

"Bloody move," I harried as we neared the reinforced glass of the door.

I shielded him as he fumbled a key into the lock. He had to open that door. Quick.

"Where are they?" He queried.

I turned my head to look. Most were scraping snow, re-loading, but two were starting towards us.

The lock click-clacked, and he was through. Thank God.

But as soon as he slipped inside, the door shut, with his body pressed against the glass. There was another click-clack.

I grabbed the handle, only to feel the resistance of a locked door. I remained stock-still, stranded.

"Ha!" came a gleeful shout from inside.

In the dull glass I could see his head cocked back in the revenge laughter I'd feigned behind Tina, the reflection of my moon-face, the small dark shapes of urban guerrillas rounding on me like a swarm of angry wasps.

"Please," I implored.

The face before me glistened with the impish delight of a child watching a Guy ablaze on Bonfire Night. Another victory, but this time with a grandstand view.

His eyes shut tight as a snowball splatted into the glass.

"Get the cunt!" a voice hollered from behind, amid a clatter of hurried footsteps.

Hands grabbed at my jacket to turn me round, a fist flew into my face.

I felt stunned, clueless what to do – then barged into the thugs, slashing away a tugging hand before fleeing towards the sports pitches, pursued by the opposition pack with its welter of expletives.

Gradually the melee petered out. Snowballs thumped around me like dud mortar shells. I slowed, then stopped to catch my breath, picturing the demonic face that would always be behind that door.

"Banks, you slag," it was hissing. "I'm the daddy around here, and don't you forget it."

The Other Side

He was in heaven again, umpiring a school cricket match – mother at square leg, black Lab sat to attention at last – when something interrupted his appreciation of an exquisite cover drive.

"Dunc," Heather whispered, jostling his shoulder under the duvet.

He tried to return to the cricket, but it had gone.

"Duncan…"

Why was she lying behind him? Oh. Holiday. France. First night. The farmhouse only had double beds.

"What?" He grumbled, voice like a bear disturbed during hibernation.

"There's someone downstairs. Listen."

He could only hear the short intakes of her breathing.

"It's probably nothing," he dismissed, "a cat or – "

A muffled bang below. He lay stock-still.

"I'm scared," she whispered again, clutching his arm. "Will you go and have a look?"

Typical. Whenever there was a problem with the house or car, he was expected to see to it even though he knew nothing about either.

He peeled back the sheet. Creaked across the floorboards. Gave an exaggerated cough. Switched on the light. Clomped downstairs. Seized a golf umbrella and brandished it like a sword. And waited.

Nothing. How ridiculous. A fifty-five year old accountant looking to take on an imaginary intruder with a brolly. Some police statement that would make.

And then he heard it – on the other side of the wall. Scratching perhaps, or grinding.

The next morning was overcast but warm enough to eat outside on the patio adjoining a can't-be-arsed kind of garden of bolted weeds and overgrown shrubs. He'd neither slept well nor raised the incident, and wanted to keep it that way. The past six months had been difficult enough; they were here to give Heather some peace and quiet after the operation. The last thing she needed was more stress.

"So what about last night?" She sought at length, blue eyes fixed on him above the empty plates.

"No idea," he replied, looking up from a map of Poitiers. "I'm sure it was nothing."

"Well it had to be *something*," she retorted, arms folded. "And it was definitely coming from there."

She glanced towards the rubblestone barn to which the nineteeth century farmhouse had been added, placing a hand across her throat.

"Maybe a pigeon got stuck," he suggested.

"A strong pigeon to have moved a plank of wood. There was a loud bang, Dunc, I swear it."

"Well, it's been and gone now, hasn't it?"

She turned away. Hopefully that was an end to it.

"Do you know," she deliberated, resuming her fixed look, "I felt uneasy the first time we came here, for John's fiftieth. Remember the story he told about the foresters who stopped for a drink of milk – and the old woman said they could have some but that the cows had TB?"

He rolled his eyes skyward and reached for his pipe.

"I know it sounds silly," she upheld, hand cradling her chin, "but the place gives me the creeps. Couldn't we sleep with the bedroom door locked tonight? Just to be on the safe side. I'd feel a lot better if we did."

"Oh, very well then," he gave in.

He went to fetch the bikes, opening the barn with a great iron key. A two-storey structure with hewn rafters. Dark. Fusty. Cool. Swags of cobwebs on the walls. Tiny droppings peppered the stone slab floor. A huge ashlar fireplace dominated the western wall adjoining the farmhouse. Late medieval, if he wasn't mistaken, possibly earlier.

The place must have served as a forge and provided a threshing floor. But now housed dust-covered junk. An ancient lawnmower. Rusting weights and scales. A disused tennis net. A pile of logs. Gardening tools. Two bicycles. Some plastic tubs of paint.

"What do you think of this crap, then?" John had joked when showing him round. "And if you get the urge to get off your backside and chop some wood, for Christ's sake don't resist it."

Duncan had always liked his brother-in-law, a retired surveyor who had bought the land for a song after chancing on it while exploring the area. It had been uninhabited since the old woman's death, then remained the only undeveloped property in the village until John's acquisition.

The barn's only openings were the fireplace and door, where the wall was nearly a metre thick. If the rest of the walls were the same width, which they had to be, the sound from the night before couldn't have carried to their room. So what had it been?

The evening darkened early and they went to bed at nine, worn out from cycling round the vineyards. Duncan locked the door, and Heather insisted the windows were kept shut, even though the air was charged.

He went to close the curtains. Iron clouds pressed against the distant hills. The horses in the paddock next door gathered by the field-gate then bolted off down the length of the fence. It seemed they knew something he didn't. And that soon the sky would crack open for gusts of rain to slash against the window and clatter across the roof tiles.

A few hours later, he heard a dull thud followed by a series of smaller ones dying away.

He opened his eyes to the darkness, and could make out that the door was open. It must have swung round and come to rest by the chest of drawers. But how? He'd locked it. Checked it. Kept the key in the door. And Heather was fast asleep; she could – would – not have opened it.

Was someone else here? He swallowed, heart thrumming, already picturing the weather-beaten face and Breton sweater of the burglar or drugs smuggler. Looked round the room – the chest of drawers indistinct, the wardrobe looming beyond the prison bars of the bedstead. But could see no one.

He'd have to close the door. If Heather woke to find it open, there'd be all hell to pay. He levered himself onto his right-hand side, but something pushed him back, confining him to where he lay. His body seemed a deadweight, unable to move. The air had soured, like the stench of rotting flesh, flowing over him from the rough wall across the landing.

He lay still, playing dead, as rain began to tinkle over the tiles. The chronic air seemed to pass. He could move again. He got up to lock the door, clambered back into bed and held onto Heather.

There was no thunderstorm, just intermittent squalls until mid-morning. They had brunch in the expanse that was kitchen, dining room and lounge rolled into one. He looked drained.

"Whatever's the matter?" Heather began across their omelettes.

"Just disappointed," he replied reluctantly, gazing at the ornate toast rack. "With the weather."

"Well, I'm glad the cycling's a wash-out. I ache all over from yesterday, don't you?"

To tell her or not? The truth would probably freak her out and negate the whole point of coming on holiday. But keeping schtum was tantamount to lying. And what if something worse happened?

She listened to his account aghast, breaths shortening.

"I'm frightened," she imparted, eyes darting towards the barn wall. "I knew something was wrong the moment we set foot in here."

"Well, we can't be sure there's a ghost here, can we?"

He checked himself, scarcely believing what he'd just said.

"Well, I am," she countered, gripping the crucifix at the base of her neck. "Think of that story about the woodmen. What if they drank the milk and died? Or contracted TB? Of course they'd still be here!"

Why had he mentioned it?

"And what about that fireplace in the barn?" She went on, almost panting. "Suppose some peasants had to undergo a trial by fire for stealing the master's corn. Or were strung up and garrotted."

He shut his eyes. It would be a satanic cult next.

"Heth, this really isn't helping."

She got up and stood by the window, holding herself with both arms, as if cold.

"I want to leave," she determined, shaking her head. "Really."

"But we've only just arrived – "

"Dunc, the place is haunted! You know it is, but as usual you're just too Mr Rational to admit it. First the banging in the barn – how do you explain that – and now this. I don't want to stay another night."

She covered her eyes with her hand, and began to cry. He got up and put an awkward arm round her, explaining the ferry ticket was non-transferable and they couldn't afford a hotel room in high season.

"Look," he angled, "whatever the problem is, it's upstairs. What if we sleep down here tonight? I can get the mattress and make up a bed. Who knows, it might be like that night in Prestatyn…"

He poked her side playfully. She looked unconvinced, dabbing her cheeks with a serviette.

"Just *one* night," he stressed. "And if anything happens, I swear to God we'll leave. All right?"

By late afternoon they were sitting in the lounge area. Duncan dozed in an armchair, a book about the Angevin monarchs on his lap. Heather sat upright in another, on guard.

And then it happened. A loud smash by the sink, followed by a clanging like a dustbin lid coming to rest.

"What was that?" He exclaimed.

Heather looked on in horror, clutching her chest, eyes flaring. He got to this feet to investigate. Glass shards, coffee granules and frying pan parts lay scattered on the terracotta tiled floor. Somehow the jar of Nescafé had fallen from the sideboard along with the old frying pan, dislodging its handle which now lay amid the debris like a blunt implement used for battering a skull.

But the objects couldn't have fallen. He'd placed the frying pan securely on top of the mugs and plates to dry, then made a coffee, pushing the jar back against the wall, a good two feet from the edge of the sideboard.

There was a tug at his shirt.

"That's it," she announced, the words bursting like air from a popped balloon. "I'm not spending another minute here. You do what you like, but I'm off. Where are the car keys?"

He checked his pockets, already following her to the French windows and out towards the sanctuary of the car.

They sat in silence, staring ahead at the rain-blotched windscreen with its drab scene of garden trees smeared against darkening sky. He ran through the incident in his mind, unable to take it in.

No point trying to explain what had happened. They just needed to get as far away as possible, as soon as possible. Whatever the cost.

But first he'd have to clear up the mess and pack their things.

He dashed back through the rain, noticing the bikes still outside from the day before. Blast. John would be livid his precious racer was contracting rust, but no matter.

Duncan crossed himself before going in and mumbled The Lord's Prayer, surprised he could remember the words.

The rain had stopped but the sky was even heavier when he returned with the suitcases and opened the boot. Heather was wiping condensation from the windows, her breathing still marked.

"Thank God for that," she muttered before resuming her look-out duty.

All he had to do now was put the bikes away, and they could leave.

The barn was almost pitch-black inside, the shapes there difficult to discern. He frisked the wall for the light switch and clicked it on. The light flickered as he jiggled the bikes inside, wedging the door open with a foot. He walked to the great fireplace and propped them against it.

The door banged shut behind him. A faint fizzle preceded a dull pop as the light went out.

He stood still, the air drained from his lungs.

In his mind he traced the route back to the door, past the logs and tennis net, and took a step forward but found himself rooted to the spot, pinned against the wall. No matter how he tried, his legs had no energy, no power. All that moved was his pounding chest.

And flowing over him, through him, that sour smell. He writhed, picturing the old crone next to him, nose pressed against his ear, sniffing, silently questioning who he was, why was he here.

Light. He needed light. To see if she was there. His matches – where were they? He tried to reach into his left pocket, but it was no good. He still couldn't move.

There was a soft pattering on the door. Rain.

He freed an arm to find the matches in his pocket. Lit one and held it aloft. Dark cobwebs hung from the walls like bats, the shadow of the log pile dragged itself closer as he moved forward. But there was no one to be seen.

On the northbound N149 to Parthenay, illuminated signs for La Rochelle and Limoges receded into the dark as oncoming headlights confirmed it was not the end of the world. Maybe the rain would hold until Rennes.

In fact, it broke before Nantes, pelting the roof with the sound of frozen peas spilling onto a hard floor, sending the wipers into overdrive. The frantic action was reminiscent of the earlier maelstrom. They stared ahead as before. Neither had spoken since leaving Sauvigny.

"Dunc," she ventured at last. "Do you think it's still with us – here, in the car?"

Sam

On any other Saturday morning in November, Geraldine would be fast asleep at her Chelsea flat or reading *The Lady* in bed with a cup of green tea, but instead was striding across a wood in a Barbour, bashing the dead bracken with a stick amid a melee of shouts and squawks while Sam bounded on ahead, flushing out pheasants towards Robert and the other Guns below.

"Whurs he, Sam?" She urged in the same way as the other beaters.

Sam stopped, snout bolted to some fallen leaves, then lunged towards a tangled clump.

"Look," Dan piped to his wiry father Ged, leading the drive, "Sam's found one."

The retriever's head rocked back in astonishment as a hen-bird darted out, barely discernible from the covert, then cluttered off to the top of the wood and away. Her heart thumped, though in truth she was relieved the bird had avoided the champagne pops of the Guns.

"Good ol Sam," Ged approved, probably encouraging her as much as him.

The irony of the situation was not lost on her. She had a fear of birds – just the thought of their snake-like eyes and quirky movements made her squirm – and abhorred killing. Geraldine could picture the looks of her lunch circle over an organic bean salad as she recounted a weekend of indiscriminate slaughter in Devon. Naturally she shared their horror, but the draw of seeing Sam in his element had proved too hard to resist.

Sam belonged to her brother Robert, a senior partner in a solicitors' practice. A pedigree retriever with a coat of golden curls and a regal demeanour easily mistaken for intelligence, any prospect of him making a gun-dog or winning Crufts had evaporated the day he was expelled from dog training for cocking his leg on the instructor then mounting an Afghan hound called Arabella.

The result was a big-hearted but unruly bear who could sit for his dinner but little else. Anyone visiting the house had to be warned that he leapt up at strangers, often pinning them to the wall. According to Robert, there were only two ways to control him. The first was to keep him on a lead outside at all times. The second, known as the *nuclear option*, for use in emergencies only, was to peel back his ear and blow down it.

"Sam absolutely hates it," he sniggered, "but he'll stop whatever he's doing immediately."

Geraldine might never have fallen for Sam were it not for her track record with men. Since Hugo's death ten years ago, she'd only been out with two, each relationship fizzling out once the novelty of her interest in rugby had worn off and the disapproval of her pig-headed sons kicked in.

After the last of these failures, she'd felt a need to get out of London, and called Robert. The subsequent trip led to her taking a shine to Mr Sambezee, who greeted the stranger in his usual manner, tail swishing with enough power to maintain the National Grid.

Geraldine visited more frequently after that, leading to Robert's suggestion that she come on a shoot.

"Sam loves it," he twinkled. "As soon as I turn off down the track for the farm, he knows exactly where he is. His ears prick up and he starts whining and drooling on the backseat. He can't wait. You'd love it, Gerrie, honestly, seeing him in action. And I promise, you won't have to touch a single bird."

Ged gave a shrill blast on his whistle to end the din of the first drive. Geraldine seized Sam to put on his chain-lead, then struggled to restrain him from pulling towards a nursery pen where the wood ended and the valley dog-legged left.

"Good ol Sam," Ged winked as the army surplus-clad beaters gathered round, obedient dogs by their sides. "He knows where them birds are, don't he boy?"

She gave a genteel smile, unsure if the question was addressed to Sam or herself.

A cock-bird scuttled out of a thicket, the white marking around its throat a collar above the autumn tweeds of the breast, squat body and long tail an ink pot and quill. She recoiled from the sudden rush of feathers as a liver-spotted spaniel dashed after it, making the bird skitter off in flight over the field.

"Come ere, you ruddy dog!" Ged ordered.

At once the dog sat still, in thrall to its master. Geraldine wondered what Sam would make of such exemplary behaviour. He was cocking his leg by a tree.

"All righ," Ged carried on. "We'll now make our way over to Denham's Copse to begin the second drive. Anyone noticed any birds thats not been picked up by the dogs below?"

"I seen one, Dad," Dan chirped. "He must ave fell some fifty yards in over there."

The boy pointed to the field on the other side of the fence.

"Righ then, genelmen," Ged resumed, "and yerself Geraldine, let's be spreadin out and get him found."

Robert had mentioned this practice of putting wounded birds out of their misery, along with other points of etiquette – that the guns are only allowed to shoot against sky and never towards the beaters. She'd felt then he was making a virtue out of the killing, but could see now he had a point.

They entered a turnip field and began walking in a line again, each ten yards apart. The dogs weaved in and out of the furrows, as the nearby wood clucked and croaked with occasional pheasant calls.

She'd always had a natural distrust of country people – silent types with green Range Rovers and a love of red meat who talked about thoroughbreds and got up far too early. But these chaps were the salt of the earth. Rough and ready. Able to command dogs. Unfazed by the sight of blood. Or feathers.

Twenty yards ahead was the dark green silk of a cock-bird's head turning like a periscope above the crop leaves. What rotten luck: the wounded bird – in her area of search. She'd have to touch it. And wring its neck. She pictured the beady eyes up close, the flapping commotion that would ensue. And squirmed.

Only the month before she'd been panicked by a starling that had fallen down the chimney. Unable to go near the sooty bird, she'd opened all the windows – panting, on edge – and waited for it to fly away. If she hadn't been able to deal with that, how the dickens could she handle this?

Hanging back from the line, she jerked Sam closer, then sank to one knee, pretending to tie a boot lace. But as soon as Sam had crossed into the same furrow, he rushed towards the pheasant, straining and gasping as if leading a sled team across the Ross Ice Shelf. He hauled Geraldine over and dragged her through the mud before she clasped the lead with both hands and managed to rein him back with a massive tug-of-war pull.

Sam raised his snout like a howitzer and started barking in great bellows, tail wagging.

"Look," Dan sang, "there he is!"

The boy walked over to the stricken bird, its head ducking below the crop leaves. Mercifully he seized it. The other beaters began to converge on him.

When she looked up, the pheasant was a throttled bundle of limp flesh and feathers in his hands.

"Ah, well done, Daniel," she blagged, off the hook, "you beat me to it."

They moved off towards the second drive – a gorse-dotted hillside that curved right and downhill back to the wood. The sun was out, and she felt surprisingly warm.

"Righ, genelmen," Ged marshalled, "an yerself Geraldine, if we're all ready. Let's be doing drive two then ave our break with their lordships down there."

He bobbed his head towards the killing zone below where the Guns stood thirty or so yards apart in Barbours and green wellies. Weapons cocked. Labradors at the ready.

There was a tug on the lead. She turned to see Sam sniffing a spaniel's bottom then mounting her, the lipstick of his penis out, eyes half closed as he started to rock back and forth on his haunches.

"Ey," Ged objected.

She yanked Sam away from another Arabella moment.

"I'm so terribly sorry, Ged," she deplored, shaking her head, "I was miles away."

"Oh, it don't matter none. He's only doing what nature intended, aren't yer boy?"

The corner of Geraldine's mouth raised in wry disapproval as she viewed her irrepressible charge, seeing now why this loose cannon of a dog had been confined to the steerage of the beaters. And why Robert had been only too happy to offload him on to her for the day.

Ged blew his whistle to begin the second drive. Geraldine unleashed Sam. He dashed straight into a bush, flushing out a hen-bird before heading downhill in a crazy-paving plan of attack known only to him. A dog possessed.

She was thinking about how to embellish the morning's trials for Robert at breaktime, and curling up with Sam by the log burner that evening, when some shouting below broke off her daydream.

A hundred yards ahead, small birds were spraying out of a nursery pen by the wood's edge and into the four corners of the universe. They were fleeing from a retriever running amok on a solo raid.

Some of the Guns were glaring at her. She started to run downhill, breaking the line. Sam hopped over the low side of the pen and padded uphill to greet her with something in his mouth. A hen-bird.

"You ruddy dog," she rebuked, unconvincingly, twenty yards away, noticing the bird's head was twitching.

Sam strolled on, head bowing this way and that with the self-aggrandisement of a crown prince acknowledging applause from both sides of a packed street during a ceremonial parade.

"Drop it," she instructed as he drew close, her forefinger pointed between his tea-dark eyes. "Drop!"

He ignored the command, tail wagging casually as the bird's eyes flitted in silent desperation.

Hell. There could be no chickening out now. She would have to touch feathers. The thought sent a shudder down her spine. She felt hot. Sick. Breathless. If only she'd brought some old gardening gloves. Or not come at all. And where the heck was Robert?

She whacked Sam on the back of the head, more in a show of strength than any belief he'd let go of his captive.

He flinched in expectation of another blow, eyes shut, but the steel trap of his jaws stayed clenched.

With both hands, she tried to prise his mouth open without touching the bird, but it was no use. Sam was not going to be parted from his trophy.

By now, all the Guns had stopped and were watching in disbelief, faces questioning whether the old girl was a saboteur or a townie. The other beaters had drawn level, some gawping at her in dismay, some looking away as if she was besmirching the reputation of their troop.

"Just wring its neck," Dan advised plainly.

"I've got a better idea," she lied.

Oh God. What would they make of this?

Geraldine knelt down on Sam's left, away from the beak that would peck out her eyes, then with one hand firmly grasping his collar, peeled back his ear flap with the other.

"What are you doing?" Dan frowned, puzzlement grooved into his face.

She took a deep breath then blew down Sam's earhole as if extinguishing candles on a birthday cake. He winced but at once released his victim, which scurried away uphill in a scrambled take-off.

Still holding onto Sam, she shut her eyes, free as the bird now winging its way over the ridge and out of sight.

Surviving Larkin

I first heard of him at the university cricket club's fundraising night at the Working Men's Club on Princess Avenue. As one by one the first eleven got up on stage to do a can-can dressed as vicars, Filth stood at a lectern reading out the poem 'Ambulances' by "that famous son of Hull, Mr Philip Larkin…"

"Who?" I mouthed to Boo over the Bad Manners soundtrack and derisive wisecracks from the floor.

"Larkin," she answered, voice raised above the din. "You must have seen him. In the library. Big, bald bloke. Wears glasses. Creepy looking."

Her housemate Sue leant forward across Boo.

"They fuck you up, your mum and dad," she warned. "They don't mean to, but they do…"

It didn't sound much like poetry to me. To my mind, a poem had be a grand effusion à la Keats or Shelley, as was the case with the odes I'd written for Boo, likening her to a skylark and a rose.

But if he could get away with having such drivel published, there was surely hope for me.

It was a cold grey morning on campus when I spotted his bald pate and black-rimmed glasses in the distance. His walk along the deserted concourse was a shuffle of caterpillar footsteps beneath a dark overcoat, head bent towards the ground, suggesting he was about to topple over at any moment.

I knew it was him because of an encounter in the library after that night out. Boo went there to keep warm between lectures, so I'd often try and lure her out to the stairwell for a snog. One afternoon I'd succeeded in prising her out to the circular balustrade on the second floor and was working on getting her to the toilet nearby, when I noticed a large, bald man on the floor below.

He was wearing a plain sixties jacket and tie, as if waiting for them to come back into fashion. His podgy white face had a hangdog expression, eyes bulging behind the thick glasses. He looked up at us, waiting for Boo to stop tittering, then raised a reverential finger to his lips before turning away.

"That's him," she noted.

"Who?"

"Your mate. Larkin."

Strange. He looked more like a monk than a poet. Not a flowing shirt or strand of long hair in sight.

I stayed put by the library entrance, knowing he must be headed there.

I still hadn't read any of his poems, which now seemed like a schoolboy error as I began to search for something to say. I could have at least checked out that *they-fuck-you-up* poem; it was bound to be in the library somewhere, and probably wasn't as bad as I'd assumed.

As he drew nearer, I walked up to him, ready to whip out some drafts from my rucksack.

"Excuse me," I started, "I understand you're a poet. I wonder if you could help – "

He carried on without even looking up.

"No," he grouched in a deep voice, the fat under his chin wobbling as he shook his head. "Very depressed today."

I looked on in shock at the back of his undertaker's coat walking away. I was a student, he was staff, I only wanted two minutes of his time. I wasn't going to read any of his poems now, that was for sure.

"Well, fuck you then!" I barked after him. "Miserable bastard."

It was hardly the laying-on-of-hands exchange I'd hoped for, and immediately I regretted the outburst – he could be ill, a relative might have died – but the words were already travelling up into the grey air, beyond anyone's reach to take them back.

Larkin carried on a few paces, as if propelled forward by the momentum of his top-heaviness, then stopped. He turned his head to the right, nodded slowly, then continued towards the library door.

Making it Happen

I saw her in the Property Valuation lecture at twelve, looking as beautiful as Mary Ure in *Where Eagles Dare*. I bottled out of approaching her then, but caught up with her group outside Pembroke. I felt sick, cold inside, unable to go through with it – but if I was going to find that partner for the May ball, this was the kind of risk I had to take.

"Excuse me," I plunged after she'd crossed the road. "Do you have the notes from that lecture?"

She and her companions looked on in bewilderment, like bunched cattle peering at a stranger through a field gate.

"I didn't get everything down," I strained, chest heaving.

I looked earnestly at her notebook, waiting for the scream of laughter. Instead, she tilted her head then gave a faint smile. Faint, that is, yet strong enough to let a thousand doves stream into the morning air.

"Oh, *that* lecture," she twigged. "No, it was the wrong one for us. We thought it was *Intellectual* Property."

"Oh. How come?"

"We are Law students from Breda. We are looking at aspects of the English legal system."

The words were so erudite, so clear. Thank God for study tours, and carrying her across the land and over the sea. But I had to keep the conversation alive. With anything.

"Law students. Breda. Right. Do you know Katherijne Verheyen?"

"No, I do not think so. Who is she?"

"Oh, a student I know. She plays hockey and tennis?"

The blank faces searched one another for knowledge of

Katherijne, and for a moment I looked among them too, joining the search. But of course they didn't know Kathy. She was at Delft, not Breda. It didn't matter: the question had bought me some time, allowing my breathing to slow.

"So, what are you doing now?" I gambled.

"Now we are going to Christ's College for lunch."

"Dey are our hosts," a tall male behind her interjected with an urgency to leave. "Ve have a schedule for our tour."

"And how long are you staying?" I returned to her, ignoring the hint. "Have you seen much of Cambridge?"

"We go back tomorrow," she replied. "We have seen a little, but I think there is a lot to see in one day. Maybe we have to come back some other time."

I looked on in alarm then resumed some indifference.

"Well, perhaps you could visit Clare College this afternoon," I gambled again. "And come to my rooms for tea? They're in Old Court. Sixteenth century. I think you might find them interesting."

She looked round at the others.

"And which college is that?" She wavered.

"It's the best."

She gave a droll smile. Then another, lowering her face. I was almost there.

"And where is that, exactly?" She deliberated.

"That-a-way," I gestured towards King's Parade.

She yabbled in Dutch with her friends.

"Maybe," she evaded. "We must go to Trinity this afternoon then to King's – for Evensong?"

"Well, it's on the way then."

She looked unsure.

"Here, let me give you my details," I offered. "I'm Scott by the way. What's your name?"

"Sventje."

"Hi," I smiled at last, writing my name and room number on a handout.

"Hi."

"Well, see you later," I handed her the note. "But no worries if not."

"Yes, maybe I will be there after four."

I smiled again then wheeled around to start towards King's, its chapel a magnificent ice palace against the arctic sky.

By four-thirty, the sky was deepening into the blue only winter afternoons can produce, and hope fading she'd come. But of course. I wasn't good-looking. Or fluent in four different languages. Whereas she was absolutely stunning. Out of my league entirely.

Besides, some slimeball from Trinity was bound to have invited her to his rooms instead.

A few footsteps clattered on the stairs, followed by three knocks. I traipsed across the floorboards, resigned to the futility of the venture, and opened the door to reveal her flawless face.

"Are you the guy I met earlier?" She inquired, puzzled.

I'd made no impression at all.

"Yeah, sure," I sank. "Come in."

She wowed at the oak timbers, then flopped into an armchair.

"So many stairs," she panted.

"Yeah, I wanted you to get some exercise."

"Don't worry. I got plenty of that already."

She declined tea and harried me about her schedule – where was Trinity, what was the time – and I asked about her course. We moved on to Holland, my stint with Auckland Council the year before and an idea for a trip to the Middle East after finals.

"What, do you have a harem there?" She teased.

"No, but some would say I was already with one of my harem."

She smiled wryly, then asked about the Boat Race, mentioning a friend was a rower.

Boyfriend, more like. And as pretty and smart as her. How I wanted to ram an oar down his throat.

"And what position does he row?" I asked.

"She rows at the front."

"She must be very good then," I rejoiced. "The best person sits at the front."

"I will tell her," she glowed. "And where do you row?"

"Right at the back."

She burst out laughing.

We covered the rest of her trip. And punting. Formal Hall. The May ball…

All too soon she was on her feet, taking in the books and pictures on my desk.

"This is your girlfriend?" She questioned, picking up a strategically positioned framed photo.

Hurrah.

"No. It's my sister actually."

"Well, thank you for entertaining me," she concluded abruptly. "I must leave now."

"No worries," I fibbed, worried she was about to disappear forever. "I'll show you where to go."

"No," she clipped, already departing. "It's OK. I can find my way. Thank you."

Of course she could. But that wasn't the point. I had to firm up something for later.

"No, really," I insisted, clomping down the stairs after her. "I'm going that way anyway."

King's Chapel loomed over us in the cold, pinnacles black beside the Delft blue, its tracery windows copperplate curls against the orange glow of the candlelight inside.

"Do you have anything planned for later?" I sought.

"Yes, we are having dinner at Trinity College."

"And after that?"

"Oh, I guess we will go for a drink somewhere."

She looked up to study the college's neoclassical facade. I studied the delicious curve of her neck.

"Well, maybe I could join you. Do you know The Champion of the Thames?"

Of course she didn't. She produced a map, and I scrawled an X to mark the spot.

"How about nine?" I chanced, breath shortening. "Or nine-thirty?"

"Maybe. I must see what the others will do."

To hell with them. Meet me alone.

"Well, let's say nine-thirty at The Champ," I rushed, then stood with hands on hips in feigned annoyance. "And if you're not there, I'll never speak to you again."

She shook her head, laughing. A good time to leave. I headed back towards Clare, remembering I'd said King's was en route to where I was going.

At nine-thirty I plodded into The Champ, rugby shirt cloying like a wet cloth, my breathing all over the place. God, how had man ever managed to mate, let alone populate the earth?

The pub was packed with young things in ski jackets, the chatter loud – and there she was, at the bar, juggling a round of drinks. Looking totally gorgeous.

"So you have bought me a beer," I lurched.

"Oh, hello. No. This is for a friend. I will take it to her."

Her nonchalance was devastating.

"You must understand," she divulged on her return, red-faced, tucking hair behind her ears. "We Dutch are careful with our money."

"It's OK. I've got some Scottish blood in me."

"Oh Scottish," she snickered, "I see."

I mentioned I was descended from Bonnie Prince Charlie and explained who he was.

"The only Prince Charlie I know is the one with big ears," she replied, raising her eyebrows, waiting for a laugh.

"Well, I'm like him," I messed, "but without the ears."

She snickered again – surprisingly – then queried why I'd brought a copy of the FT.

"I have an interview with the Diplomatic Service next week."

"That is interesting. My father works for the International Court of Justice in The Hague."

I couldn't believe my luck.

We sat down as she explained his role and that she did some part-time modelling.

"Yeah, I do that too," I sighed.

"Aha."

"I mean models of ships in bottles. That kind of modelling?"

"Well," she grinned, getting it, "I think you could be a model too."

Kapow.

"What – they need ugly people too, eh?"

She looked at me, shining, and held the gaze. We were on a different footing now. And even I knew it.

After the bell for last orders, she agreed to go to Don Carlo's for a coffee. We descended into its brick-vaulted basement and sat at a small table with a red tulip at its centre.

"Tulips," I contemplated profoundly, trying to sound learned, "do you know the poem by Sylvia Plath?"

"No, I have not read her works."

Her works. The phrase sounded so studious, so sweet.

"But I do know another poem about flowers," she leant forward. "Shall I quote it for you?"

"Please do."

"Shall I compare you to a summer's day?" She began. "No, you are more lovely, and more temperate."

She gave an uncertain smile, waiting for me to guess the poet.

"I know that," I frowned. "Keats, isn't it?"

Her face straightened in disappointment.

"Let me give you a clue," she added. "It's something to do with you."

Think, you idiot, think. My neck swarmed with heat.

Then it hit me. Someone as lovely as a summer's day was comparing *me* to one. Wasn't she? No, she couldn't be. Yet she must be. Or was I reading too much into it?

"I'm sorry," I stalled, dying in flames. "I can't think straight. John Donne?"

Her smile disappeared again. I was failing her.

"Stratford?" She cued with a blank look.

"Oh, Shakespeare," I clocked, lolling my tongue like an exhausted dog. "At last."

The most wonderful smile beamed back, Ingrid Bergman and Kim Bassinger rolled into one.

"Of course, how stupid of me," I admitted. "Which play is that?"

Her face straightened again.

"It's not a play," she rebuffed. "It's a sonnet."

Disaster. I'd only started with literature to impress her

– yet here I was floundering, drowning in the shallows. I looked down, crushed again, but this time made no attempt to hide it. I'd always wanted someone special to share poems with, and here she was. And here I was, screwing everything up.

She went to the ladies, perhaps sensing something was wrong. I lowered my head then thudded it against the table as if hammering in a nail.

So this was love. That sunken feeling in the stomach. The hopelessness, imbalance, despair.

But somehow I had to get it on. I took a napkin and wrote out Whitman's "Poem".

"That's really beautiful," she purred on her return. "Thank you."

I tried to take a mental picture of her face, in case I couldn't remember it once she'd left, noting the simplicity of her straight hair and lack of make-up. It was hard to think of her as a model somehow.

Hard too not to think of her reclining in a punt during the musky light of an evening in June, with me plumbing a pole into the gravelly river bed, at last feeling no need for words.

Outside, the night was a glistening coalmine. A film of rain covered the cobbles of the market place, the iron hands of the City Hall's clock clunked to XII like an old pair of garden shears.

"Most colleges lock their gates at midnight," I warned, breath smoking into the air. "If you can't get into Christ's, you can always stay at my place."

"No," she stopped.

"No, I mean – "

"Scott, which is the way for me, please?" She demanded.

"Well, it's that way," I pointed towards Lion's Yard, "but – "

"It's OK, I can walk on my own."

She set off without me.

"Yes, but this is Cambridge," I wriggled, catching up, "it's a dangerous place."

"What?" She stopped again. "Cambridge – dangerous?"

"Sure. Well, it is with me around."

Her incredulity gave way to that wry smile. I was back in the game.

We headed towards the Earth Sciences building in silence.

I wanted to touch her, hold hands, and felt she might not reject my touch. I certainly didn't want her to think of me as just some literary pen-pal. I wanted her, and wanted her to know it.

As we passed the Corn Exchange, I realised we'd soon be approaching Christ's. This was where it ended and I turned back into a pumpkin.

Should I try to kiss her, that was the question. What if she spurned the advance? What did she want? A peck on the cheek would be the safe option, a gentlemanly gesture even, but a total cop-out too. *Play safe*, ordained a voice inside my head. *Live*, raged another.

I stopped her outside the Columbas United Reform Church.

"Look, Sventje," I started, pointing a finger at her belly-button then resting it on her jacket. "Despite appearances, I'm a wonderful guy, and you're extremely lucky to meet me."

Her lips parted into a grin, eyes sparkling in the cold, body easing back against the wall. This was it. I edged closer, tugging her towards me. Her face neared mine. I looked down at her lips, then back to her eyes as I placed my top lip above hers. I shut my eyes and kissed her gently.

As I drew my head away, her bottom lip came away with mine, momentarily, as if glued. I gave an embarassed smile, and so did she. It had been just right.

"I've really enjoyed meeting you, Sventje."

"Me also."

I looked at the most perfect girl I'd seen, let alone touched, kissed. And to think that morning we'd not even met. It was my greatest achievement, yet I hadn't really achieved anything.

"You will write, won't you?" I checked.

"Yes, I will."

She turned to cross the road into the college. And was gone.

Not *That* Yellow, Vincent

Bruce sometimes describes the way Vini's other manager treats Vin as being like someone peering over Van Gogh's shoulder and shouting, "No, not that yellow, you dick, this yellow."
– Tony Wilson, Factory Records

Good things come to those who wait. This I know from waiting twenty years to go to a gig by The Durutti Column, then not only see them live in Manchester but meet guitarist Vini Reilly. For over a week I buzz with first love, daydreaming of meeting Little Vin again.

Back at work, a colleague familiar with my *grand passion* hands me an article from the Evening News with a picture of someone resting his head against the neck of a guitar held upright by a frail, wizened hand. It is Vini, gazing towards the agony column like a romantic poet.

Vini Reilly makes works of genius and is hailed the world over, it begins, *so why did he become destitute and have a brush with death?*

I devour the article at speed, learning he was one of five children raised on a council estate in Wythenshawe. His father, a pianist, didn't allow a TV in the house, so Vini spent his time playing piano and football, excelling at both. Aged twelve, he was offered a place at the Northern College of Music to become a concert pianist; aged fifteen, trials with Man City.

But Vini's destiny lay in a different kind of blues. He swapped piano for guitar, and later still punk for the meditative sounds of The Durutti, signing for Factory Records (so called because so many factories were closing that founder Tony Wilson liked the idea of one opening) before gaining a fervent following in guitar-mad Portugal and critical acclaim in England. Brian Eno even cited *LC* as his favourite album.

Then Factory fell apart. A huge tax demand forced the guitarists' guitarist to sell his flat and left him with nothing. He contributed to works by Morrissey (though this spell as a hit-maker "bored me terribly"), but his mother's death and the constant struggle with illness and depression took its toll. He became a heroin addict, with debts no musician could pay. At one point, a hitman pointed a gun at his head to force payment.

"Pull the trigger," Vini told him. "I don't care."

Clearly his had hardly been the life of Reilly.

Vini's troubles trouble me. I think of how his music has enriched my life, and want to help. Not for the first time, I wish I was fantastically wealthy, able to hire the starving artist to play all night and buy him a meal, house, anything.

Then again, I've already done much for the cause. I've bought Vini's vinyl for my family and friends, in part as insurance in case I wear mine out, in part to prepare them for my funeral, but also to stick a few quid in Vini's pocket and keep the sacred flame alive. Buying sixteen CDs at a Virgin Megastore one Monday morning even resulted in The Durutti topping the LP sales chart for half an hour.

There's only one thing I can do for Vini now – help promote his new album, *Someone Else's Party*. I cannot denounce it as the work of the devil and burn copies in a public place, but I can persuade – coerce, blackmail – my DJ mate Jon to interview Vini on his radio show.

Two weeks later, at 6.26pm on Sunday 18th May, I'm pacing up and down outside Jon's studio on the corner of Leicester Square, having bought him a ticket to the Durutti gig at Ronnie Scott's that night if he'll interview Vini on his show. Outside, there is no sign of the Vinimania that should greet my unlikely hero.

"Typical," Jon tuts during an ad break, "these let-downs happen all the time in the music business."

As if on cue, in walks Vini accompanied by a huge slab of a black security man and a Brazilian-looking beauty with a clipboard. For someone down on his luck, he does not seem to be doing so badly.

Vini looks like a cross between Dustin Hoffman and Keith Richards, only smaller and more skinny. He's wearing shabby army surplus clothes, several sizes too big, as if bought for him to grow into. He looks more like a *Big Issue* seller than a rock god, and stares up at us in a haunted way.

He disappears with the girl into the studio, an Orpheus descending into the underworld. The bouncer stays by my side, as if forewarned to restrain me from rushing in and squeezing Vini to death or grabbing the microphone to call for his birthday to be made a national holiday. He squashes into the white sofa opposite to read a muscle mag while 'Sketch for Dawn' begins to throb from the internal sound system.

"That sound," I muse. "Incredible. You know I'd rather see The Durutti than a world cup final."

The bouncer nods, chewing gum, but quickly returns to his mag. He's probably never heard of The Durutti before today and will have forgotten them by tomorrow.

"You're listening to Jon K, with you til eight, and tonight we've got a very special guest," Jon declares as the track fades. "He's one of the finest guitarists in the world. He's rocked the Manchester and British music scenes for thirty-five years. He's a living legend. And his name is Vini Reilly."

My heart is in my mouth. Will the lamb I just saw live up to his billing?

"Vini, welcome to the show," Jon carries on, shifting to a conversational tone. "It's great to have you here, and great you're still making music."

"Mm, thanks," Vini mumbles, voice barely there. "I think it's just that I didn't die."

Jon laughs politely, Vini nervously.

"That was Vini's band, The Durutti Column," Jon tells his invisible audience. "'Sketch for Dawn', from the album *LC*, which was the first Durutti track I fell in love with, a long time ago. When did it come out?"

There is a long pause.

"Um," Vini stumbles. "I've no idea…"

"1979, 1980?"

"Eighties," Vini butts in. "1980-somethin. It was done on a 4-track reel-to-reel in a jingle studio. And the new album was done on an 8-track Portastudio… So, all these years later, I'm still doin my own thing. It's quite weird."

I balk at the techno-speak, which will be incomprehensible to the average listener. It is hardly the best start.

Jon covers Factory, Eno and Morrissey. Then asks for Vini's take on the Manchester music scene.

"I don't know," Vini gulps. "I don't really socialise with other musicians. I tend to inhabit my own small world… Which is a bit sad, I suppose. The only time I step out of it is when I do gigs and stuff."

An opportunity missed to plug his band, record, life. I sense the frustration Tony Wilson must have felt at his protégé's unrivalled ability to score ten out of ten for production but a big fat zero for marketing. No wonder his management of Vini was once likened to someone shouting at Van Gogh, *No, not that yellow, you dick, this yellow.*

Jon touches on early influences, bringing Vini out of his shell, before moving on to the new album.

"Vini, you've been quoted as saying this is the only album you think has been worth putting out."

"Yeah. I think, you know, if a pass is, like, 45 per cent or something, then this is the first one to hit that mark thing."

I wince at the disparaging of everything he's done. Who will buy *LC* now? Even the bouncer looks up and rolls his eyes towards the ceiling.

"I'm amazed you say that because you've made some magical albums. Is that what keeps you going – challenging yourself to hit the mark?"

"I think so. I want to make just one really good album… Before I die. But it's not happened so far. This last one is OK, but it's not that good really…"

I shake my head at his lack of commercial awareness, his lack of self-belief. *No, not that yellow, you dick,* I can hear myself saying, over and over again.

At last, Vini emerges, a caged bird set free, and walks up to me.

"You must be Jon's friend," he guesses, head tilted to one side, "the one who set up the interview?"

"Yes, that's me."

"Thank you," he smiles, extending a hand. "I really app-reciate it."

"No, no. *Thank you.* For the music, I mean."

I look down at the floor, face and ears burning.

"Don't I know you?" He gawps, mouth ajar like a child wondering at fairy lights.

"Well, sort of. We met in Manchester. At your last gig."

"Oh yeah," he reflects, continuing his stare. "Will, isn't it?"

I'm speechless. He has remembered my name.

"Well, thank you, Will. I'm really grateful. It's been a big honour bein here."

"No, no, the honour's all mine, really."

Another wave of heat torches my face.

"Are you comin to the concert tonight?" He asks, laying a wizened hand on my forearm.

"Of course. Wouldn't miss it for the world."

"Well, come backstage for a beer afterwards. You and Jon. It'd be really good to see you."

Backstage. I've always wanted to go backstage, to experience that rock and roll vibe. It's too good to be true, and seems like destiny. Twenty years of nothing – then seeing the great one twice in two weeks. It must be my mother's doing in heaeven.

"Vini," the Brazilian beauty intervenes, "I am sorry but we have to go."

I give an understanding smile as she whisks him away, the bouncer plodding behind.

Jon claims the table reserved for him at Ronnie Scott's while I get the beers in, ready for an evening of speed-drinking, anything.

Miss Brazil is sitting at the next table with some middle-aged men in open-necked shirts and suits.

"Record company execs," Jon remarks quietly.

And with them, small and innocuous in the corner, is the real star. I have to see him. I lope across the floor and sit next to Vini before anyone else can claim the sacred space.

"Hi Vini, do you want a drink?" I broach.

"No… It's OK…"

The words are scarcely audible, his hangdog expression as miserable as Mancunian rain.

"Are you OK?"

"I just don't understand why all these people are here."

He stares at the floor, condemned again.

"They're here because they love your music. They want to see you play."

"But all my music is rubbish," he mutters, getting up to head backstage. "Except one or two tracks from the last album, which aren't as rubbish as the rest."

Despite the rapturous applause, Vini walks to the microphone like a dog walloped for no reason, almost dwarfed by the stratocaster he is clutching in both hands. I can barely watch.

"Ello," he starts. "Thank you for comin tonight. Usually at the start of a concert I get really nervous about makin mistakes. But then this place is jazz, so I suppose anythin goes."

There is a ripple of laughs. Thank God the joke has worked.

Vini bows his head to focus on the guitar. The spotlight creates a lilac-blue shadow under the strap, just as it did in Manchester. It seems he is the only person in the room. And then he begins to pluck some delicate notes from the instrument, each one flowering into the night, as if drawing every bird and animal from its nest or lair.

I take in his delectable, spiralling guitar and occasional *sotto voce* – sometimes with my eyes shut, in deep devotion, at others wide awake, flicking my pocket with an imaginary plectrum. The set is vintage Vin, and I am ready to follow him anywhere.

"I feel guilty being here," Jon confesses between tracks. "I don't see enough of Em and Jack. Em took him to the park recently, and he asked, *Mummy, why do those children have a daddy with them?* You can imagine how I felt."

"So what did Em say? *It's because your Daddy has had to get pissed with his mates again?*"

We burst out laughing, back at uni once more.

A hand is thrust my way from one of the record company executives.

"Hello, I'm Justin," he introduces himself with a trace of Eton or Harrow.

I notice Miss Brazil smiling at us over his shoulder. Hopefully he has come to say she wants to meet me, rounding off this crystal day.

"We've been enjoying watching you watch Vini. And Alicia tells me you set up the radio interview this afternoon, which I'd like to thank you for."

"Pleasure. Anything for Vini. His music is the soundtrack to my life. I love it."

I shut my eyes as Vini begins 'The Missing Boy', the band's signature tune about Ian Curtis, the Joy Division frontman and former Factory stablemate who killed himself aged twenty-three.

"That's why I wanted to have a word," he goes on. "We're thinking of putting together a compilation CD of the best Durutti tracks and wondered if you could come up with a running order for us."

Oh Jesus, thank you. Clearly there is a God after all.

We visit the slender genius backstage after the gig. I am surprised how easy it is to walk into the room where the band is signing posters and unwinding. As Jon begins to chat to them, I notice Vini sitting alone in a corner. He looks shattered.

"Hiya," I sidle up to him. "You OK?"

He registers my presence like a dormouse stirring from sleep.

"Yeah. Just knackered."

"Well, you were brilliant tonight. Fantastic."

"I wasn't that good... But thank you. And thank you for everythin this afternoon."

"Oh, it's nothing. Actually, I've got something for you."

I hand him two letters in sealed envelopes – one with condolences about his mother's death, with poems attached, the other asking if I can write a book about his life.

"Don't open them now, but later," I suggest, "I'm not the best talker, so find it easier to get things across on paper. A bit like you on guitar perhaps..."

He angles his head and gives me that look of innocent wonder.

"You will read them, won't you?" I ask.

"Yeah, I will... I'm just sorry I'm so tired... It'd be really nice to go for a coffee or somethin sometime, just you and me, back in Manchester. Have a proper chat."

He turns with a slow smile, and the exchange of glances makes me feel good. So good I can't stop myself from putting an arm round him and squeezing his tiny frame – then let go in case his bones snap.

Jon and I leave by the stage door, entering the dark of the deserted street. Above us, the pock-marked face of a half-moon resembles a cue ball partially obscured by the black.

I've always been grateful that Vini's life coincided with mine and now feel privileged, relieved, elated to have seen him live, thanked him, helped him even. And to think he singled me out at the radio station, suggested we go for a coffee. And that I might be selecting tracks for the compilation – *The Least Worst of The Durutti Column* – and maybe even writing his biography – *Hardly The Life of Reilly.* It is too good to be true.

Everything seems enchanted – London, life, even the littered street – and I feel the surge of happiness that comes only once or twice a lifetime. In fact, I'm so happy I could cry.

I'm a northerner though, and we have to get back to Jon's. He hails a cab as I try to regain some composure and focus on making some notes for that story about Vini.

But then it wouldn't be good enough. Because all my stories are rubbish. Except the one or two which aren't as rubbish as the rest.

Seeing Him Again

Which way home? The way you ran to Tracey's, along the flyover? Or the shortcut by the canal then over the foot-bridge and through the estate? The light's OK but it'll be dark in half an hour. You don't want your mum fretting, and if you get home after nine, Dad'll only think you've been with a boy. It's got to be the shortcut.

You can't risk a calf strain with the county trials next week-end, so you do some stretches then jog from Tracey's door, trainers clapping over the wet tarmac, red nylon tracksuit flashing past in the windows of the Minis and Ford Cort-inas parked along Dore Street.

The down-at-heel town stretches out below in places you've known all your life. The Victorian library. St Mary's steeple. The old gasworks site. Terraced houses with lights on. Terraced houses with lights off, a blue-grey glimmer downstairs as that mournful trumpet signals the end of *Coronation Street*.

You focus on your pace and breathing, but the bridges come to mind. Granddad used to say they were guarded by trolls when you were little. And they still are. Trolls that smoke weed and steal cars. Trolls with dads who have done time. It's their manor when you cross the railway bridge – and Gail Barton is bound to be hanging out there some-where with her mates.

You slow down and walk up its metal grate steps, noticing a train scuttling off up the line into the twilight, wheels sparking intermittently like a cigarette butt flicked out of a speeding car.

You tread softly. As you near the top, the asphalt of the high-sided walkway comes into view. All clear. You can't see over the sides, so it feels like you're in a tunnel. Halfway across you hear footsteps clunking up the other side. Is it them? You stop, thinking of your escape route back, whether they'd be quick enough to catch you.

An old couple round the corner. Both are wearing heavy overcoats and thick black NHS specs.

"By eck," the man wheezes on seeing you. "Wor I wouldn't give for the legs of a young un."

You give a polite smile, unsure how to reply.

"All righ luv," he winks as you pass. "Just wotch yersen."

You start running again, down Water Lane, your back warm and moist now. Barton's gang could be at the footbridge – ready to trip you up, barge into you. You think about going back, but you'd have to overtake the old couple. Which would make you look lost or silly. Or both.

You pass the last streetlight and turn right onto the towpath. The stagnant water has a dank smell. It's years since you were last here, brambling with Grandma, and the briars have grown into a wire mesh festooned with rotten cigarette packets and used condoms.

Tracey's mum comes back to you from earlier.

"Sure you don't want a lift, Katie?" She checked as Tracey slouched by the door.

"No, it's all right, Mrs F," you demurred, trying to sound adult. "Thank you."

"Or phone your mum? Let her know you're on your way?"

"I'm fine. Really."

But you're not. Darkness is filling the canal as a slight breeze causes the branches to sweep the dishwater sky. You can see bats zig-zagging above the waterway, but the light is murky, hampered by the large mills on the right and the mature trees lining both banks. The place is alien. You shouldn't be here.

Something scutters in the briars. A rat? There must be thousands of them here. What if they all came teeming across the towpath now? What would you do?

Barton returns to mind.

"Why don't you just leave her alone?" You'd protested when she called Tracey a slag that morning. Immediately, her bulky face was up close and personal in yours.

"And why dunt yer piss off McKenzie?" She waded in. "Just cos your dad as two cars, yer think yer better than us, dunt yer?"

Mrs Holroyd had entered the classroom then. But out here there's no Mrs H, no bell to end a fight. Out here it's just dogshit and discarded cans. And you're the system, the state. A target.

Eighty yards ahead is the dull glow of a lamp attached to an old mill. It's the last light before the footbridge, some four hundred yards away. You remember a news story about a nurse who was raped on her way back from a night shift. What if you were attacked? Would anyone hear your shouts? Or bother to do anything?

You run faster. But the path is muddy in places, and only a yard wide. You'd forgotten it was this narrow, and can't risk falling in. Besides, the block-stones on the edge of the canal are a good two or three feet above the water. If you fell in, how would you get out?

You look up at the lamp as you pass. Its rusted iron fitting must predate the First World War. For a moment the light blinds you. You stop, blinking to regain your sight, breathing hard. Can't see a thing. Then you hear the scrunch of footsteps on clinker.

You squint into the gloom. Fifty yards ahead is the glowing orange tip of a cigarette. A stocky male figure. He has a mane of dark wavy hair, like a thick-set version of Jim Morrison, and looks vaguely familiar, but maybe this is wishful thinking. You start jogging again – to show no fear – on the inside edge of the path so he can't push you in. Your heart is racing.

"Katie!" he hails, about thirty yards away.

You slow down and walk, racking your brains to think who he could be.

"It's young Kate, isn't it?" He inquires with an uncertain smile as you draw near.

You stare at him, gobsmacked. It's Carl, Paula's brother. You once cleaned his Norton with her for 50p before he set off in leathers to a T. Rex concert with his biker mates.

He draws the cigarette to his face and takes a drag like some dude in a western.

"Where yer off ter?" He grins as a veil of smoke wafts across his face.

"Oh, I'm just on my way home," you laugh nervously, already scarlet.

"Well, dunt go ter footbridge. There's a load of lads an lasses waitin for yer."

He flicks some ash towards the canal.

"Just get yersen back onta main road."

"Ah, cheers Carl. See yer."

You turn and head back the way you came, thinking how weedy you sounded, that you've never said *yer* in your life before. But thank God you're avoiding the footbridge and will be returning under streetlights. Though you're going to be in for it when you get back home.

You run back uphill to Tracey's then left onto the main road. The streetlights cover the pavement in a soft yellow pall. You know you should stop at hers and call your mum, but you're moving now like never before. As if you're flowing, not running. And could go on forever.

You laugh. Carl of all people. In the last place you'd expect him to be. He must be seeing a girl on the estate. You think how beautiful she must be and what it must feel like on his motorbike – arms clasped around his hulking body, hair streaming behind.

You run on, fists clenched, trainers caked in mud, slowing briefly at the flyover. Sure enough, a gang is at the footbridge, caught in an arc of light from the estate a hundred or so yards to your left. Some girls are leaning over the bridge, a boy is showing off on a rusted Chopper, and another is pissing into the canal.

The next day you're buzzing. Can't wait to go to school. You've been thinking about Carl all night, and have remembered an incident with him the year before. It was the day after Lee Shipton swore he'd kick Paula's head in. You'd just got off the bus when you heard Carl behind.

"Shipton," he beckoned, "I wanna word wi you. Our kid says yerve threatened er. Well, I've got news for yer. If yer lays a finger on er I'm gonna come round an sort yer out. Gerrit?"

Lee looked as if he was about to wet himself. He never went near Paula again.

Up until the previous evening, Carl was just the blur of a friend's man-boy brother; but now he is a knight in dull armour who will protect you from evil. You've got to tell Tracey about it. And get Paula to thank him. But most of all you just want to see him again. Run past the gym where he works, even, after school.

There's no sign of Paula in assembly, and Tracey arrives

late, tucking herself into the space you've saved as everyone stands to sing "All Things Bright And Beautiful".

The singing dies away. Everyone sits. A cough echoes from the back of the hall.

"I'm afraid I have some sad news," Mr McKendrick announces. "One of our former pupils, Carl Davies, the brother of Paula Davies, was killed in a road accident yesterday afternoon. Naturally, Paula will not be attending school for a while, and our thoughts are with…"

Your breathing falters. It feels as if someone has kicked you in the stomach.

But he can't have died yesterday afternoon because he was with you in the evening. The news is wrong. You can smell the canal, picture his face in the murky light. Carl was standing next to you as sure as Tracey is now. Wasn't he? And if it wasn't Carl, then who was it?

No. He knew your name. It was Carl. Definitely. And you'd said, "cheers Carl" or something like that. If it wasn't Carl, he'd have said that wasn't his name.

So who – what – did you see, speak to?

You have no idea. You believed in ghosts and angels as a little girl, but have recently figured out such things can't exist. So what do you believe now?

You should feel scared, but all you can think of is that you're never going to see him again. Never going to say *thank you*. You want to cry.

McKendrick is still talking. Everyone bends forward in a mass shuffle except you. You're staring at the tiny stars of dust caught in the sunbeams flooding through the long windows, obscuring a figure at the side of the hall. You can't see the face, but can just about make out the wavy hair.

It is some time before you register McKendrick's words. He has just said, "Let us pray."

That Friday

"You are up late," she glared while dusting the grand piano, the voice accentless, the activity at odds with her silver perm and pearls. "I suppose you want a cooked breakfast."

"It's OK, Mrs Sondberg, thank you – "

"No, it is no trouble. You English always say no when you mean yes."

We were back to the day before, when she'd ridiculed my view that Sventje should leave home then flicked a switchblade finger to command, *Do not plan your life around my daughter – you think you know her, but you don't.* Sventje had walked in then, her mother asking softly if she'd like some strawberries in the garden. But this morning there was no Sventje to walk in and break the curse. I had a whole day to get through.

I helped myself to some orange juice on the table and sat by the framed poster of some pretty boy giving Sventje a rose. I'd never liked it.

"I enjoyed debating the third world with Isaac last night," I lied, making conversation.

I pictured him the evening before, scoffing at my attempt to learn Dutch, disrupting everything I said.

"You are an idealist, Scott," she proclaimed without looking up. "When you are older, you will think differently because you will have had experience. What will you do in life? Work in Africa?"

If only I'd gone into Breda with Sventje.

"No, I don't think so. I'm – "

"See what you think in a few years. People become less

idealistic with time."

She returned to keeping the house just so. Perhaps I should try another angle.

"Actually," I confided, starting to clear the table for her, "it's quite nice to have a day off from Sventje."

"That's funny," she smirked. "She said the same thing this morning."

She scanned the floor with a dark smile, showing her true colours again.

Oh, sod it. I made for the door to walk round the block in the September sun. And get some air.

I'd met Sventje earlier that year at Cambridge. She was beautiful, cultured and Dutch. Seemed strong and independent, like my former sweetheart Katherijne. I invited her to the May ball and she came, even hinting that partners one day got married. We visited Oxford and Stratford. Watched *Hamlet* and *Romeo and Juliet*. Went punting and cycling. And made love in a wheat field by the Cam. It was her first time, aged twenty-five.

Things had gone well when I stayed with her family in July and she came to meet mine in August. I'd never known such happiness, believed she was the one and that she felt the same, often telling me *ik hou van jou*. I also thought her father was great, despite Sventje sending me an Ogden Nash poem beforehand in which the speaker dreams of the infanticide of his daughter's future suitor.

But shortly after our first kiss, she broke down about her brother Andre. He'd slashed his wrists the week before, after a family meal to celebrate his twenty-ninth birthday, and was now looking for a place of his own. No one seemed to know why, so I vowed to find out – to help him, and save her.

This proved impossible when I agreed to the mother's request never to discuss it with him. Which made me think the attempt was linked to her plea, *What will I do,* when bemoaning the possibility of her *children* leaving home. And the fact that she'd run away aged fifteen, never to contact her own mother again.

I returned to the tiny back garden enclosed by a tall hedge, sat at the table and opened the Dutch textbook Sventje had given me. I'd show the father… The mother came out to sit opposite, face stiffened, then rolled up her sleeves and leant forward into my personal space, studying me. I pretended to read, heart punching out of my chest, breaths faltering.

"Scott, are you still angry with me?" She prickled, mouth simmering with derision.

"Still?" I questioned, sitting back a little. "I'm not angry with you, Mrs Sondberg. Upset perhaps, but not angry."

My face swarmed with heat.

"Yes, you are, I can see it," she goaded, shifting in her chair. "But why? What have I done? Was it something I said?"

"Well, to be honest, you dismissed my view on something earlier without hearing me out."

The reason sounded so trivial now it was out in the open.

"So?" She mocked. "What I think is not so important."

"Yes, it is. It's very important."

"Phhh!" she whinnied, as if I'd just suggested the world was flat. "Rubbish, Scott."

My eyes sank. What had I done to deserve this?

"No," I countered. "What you think is very important to me. Mr Sondberg and Andre too."

Her powdered face straightened, eyes welling. A tear ran down her left cheek to cling to the base of her jaw, a diamond above pearls, then fell, dotting her black polo top like a raindrop.

"But why?" She snuffled.

"Because of Sven, of course. What her family thinks affects the way she sees me."

"No!" she spat, tears flowing freely. "I do not say, *Sventje, he is bad*, so Sventje thinks that. She has her own mind – I am not her mummy who tells her, *do this, do that.*"

"Oh, come on," I remonstrated. "We are all affected by what our parents think. I know if my mother – "

"Shhh," she quashed, glancing towards the house next door. "But why is it so important what Sventje thinks of you?"

I looked down again, stranded. If only this was being filmed – Sventje might not believe it otherwise.

"Why, Scott? Why do you like her so much?"

Her tone was emotionless, face gun-barrel straight. The gloves were off, there was no need to play the polite hostess with her daughter gone for the day.

"What do you think of her, Scott?"

Perhaps she thought I just wanted Sventje for sex.

"Well, I think the world of her. Why else take her to the May ball? I mean, a ticket costs over – "

"Money?" She shouted, face distorted in disgust. "What is this talk of money? You think you can buy her, do you?"

I stood up.

"Right," I asserted, pointing at her, Dutch-style. "That's enough."

"So you think my daughter is rubbish," she recoiled, "is that it?"

"How dare you?" I rebutted, face hardened. "I've never been so insulted in my life."

I turned to leave, muttering *Good God* within earshot. But feeling I'd done what needed to be done.

I went upstairs to Sventje's room and sat on the double-bed, head in my hands, chest heaving. Outside, the blue sky was just as I'd left it, a bird chirping in the same way as a few minutes before. And yet, within those few minutes, everything had changed.

Why hadn't I gone into Breda? Right now I could be sitting outside a café watching the girls go by while Sventje did her viva at the university. None of this would have happened. And there was probably more to come.

I remembered how we'd returned the evening before, after making love in the woods – the odd way the mother had looked up from a clandestine conversation with the father at the table then slid away without a word. Clearly I'd been the subject of debate. And wasn't good enough for her. But why not? What more could I have done?

I looked at the camp-bed inserted between Sventje's bed and window for me to sleep on. I was sick of the sight of it. Sick too of waiting for the mother to switch on the dishwasher before Sventje and I could make love. Her entering immediately afterwards for our washing. Her fussing over Sventje like a pampered doll. Her arranging photo shoots for Sventje when I only had a few days left. Her pooh-poohing my belief that Sventje should leave the mothership. Her emotional blackmail to ensure Sventje never did. Her ban on any meaningful discussion with Andre. Her order not to plan my life around Sventje. And now this.

On the wicker chair by the bottom of the bed sat a neat pyramid of folded T-shirts, pants and socks the mother had ironed. I rose to turf them out onto the floor, then grabbed my orange rucksack and shoved it upright in the chair. There were footsteps on the stairs then a knock on the door.

"Scott, can I have a moment, please?" She requested.

The honeyed tone could not have been more different to

that only minutes before.

"No," I smarted, twisting a pressed shirt as if wringing it dry. "You cannot."

She came in anyway, face stained with mascara like a witch in an amateur performance of *Macbeth*. I took aim then hurled the shirt into the rucksack.

"What are you doing?" she gasped, right hand clasped across her chest.

"Take a wild guess."

"You are leaving?"

She sank back against the wall as I strode towards the landing.

"But why, Scott? What have I said? You put thoughts in my mouth that do not exist – "

"Bullshit!" I blazed as I headed into the bathroom. "So, why all the questions then – about Sventje?"

She shied away from me, eyes shut.

"Why?" She jabbed, as I came out with my toothbrush. "What is wrong with that?"

"Wrong? It's none of your bloody business, that's what's wrong."

I returned to the bedroom and threw the toothbrush at the rucksack but missed.

"Please," she fretted, half-entering, half-biting her bottom lip. "Don't leave. I shall make some coffee. Come downstairs and talk."

She left, shutting the door behind her. I sat on the bed staring at the rucksack. I didn't want to leave Sventje, or risk her thinking badly of me. And shouldn't have sworn. And this was her mother. She'd had a hard childhood, but had taken action to make something out of her life. Besides, what was she doing now? Making coffee? Calling the father at the office? Or reaching for Andre's knife?

She was standing near the piano, a dark figure in a darkened room, cheeks streaked with tears. There was a noble defiance about her, like a captured queen. I went outside to collect my book from the table.

"Please, Scott," she started on my return inside. "Can we talk? Please."

She was wringing her hands, bottom lip quivering.

"I don't understand you," she went on, mouth contorting. "Or why Sventje is so special to you."

She pulled a white handkerchief from a sleeve and buried her face in it with both hands, crying.

"It is so sad, so sad," she erupted, shaking her head. "You and she are so in love!"

The words jolted through me, making no sense.

"Sorry?"

"Sventje," she hoarsened, "she is so young, so inexperienced."

I stared at the floor, trying to absorb the remarks, as she clutched her stomach then broke down again, wailing something in Dutch.

"Sorry?" I repeated.

"If Isaac goes with another woman," she wept bitterly, a hand drawn across her face, "I know he will come back."

Oh no. She didn't deserve this. But why tell me, here, now? And how did this relate to Sventje and me?

"Yes," I struggled, thrown.

She leant against the wall, burying her face once more, crying uncontrollably. I felt dazed, as if reeling from a punch, skin burning up again. In my mind a curtain began to be drawn against the sky.

"That's why I've said if Sven wants to go with another, it's OK," I added lamely.

She shook her head vehemently, then withdrew the

handkerchief from her face, eyes closed.

"But what is so sad?" I asked, stupefied, touching the back of a chair for support.

She shook her head again, disowning the thought like a defector who has already said too much, her face melting in another wave of grief.

Poor woman. I stepped forward to hug her, placing a hand on her right shoulder – but she shrank back, as if I were a killer. I advanced again with open hands – but she shielded her face with hers, digging my grave deeper.

"Look, Mrs Sondberg," I ventured, stepping away. "I think we should have that coffee, don't you?"

At last she uncovered a pouting face, and nodded.

We reconvened in the cool of the main room. She handed me a coffee in the best china, with a butter biscuit on the saucer, then tucked her grey worsted skirt behind before perching on the edge of the black sofa.

"You must understand Scott," she began. "Sventje is so special. So special to me. Not just because she is so beautiful. All our friends say she is special. Even at school, she was more special than all the other children."

She dabbed her face with the handkerchief, eyes glistening.

"And please understand another thing," she continued. "When Andre was born, it was the best thing that happened in my life. To have a little boy, it was so wonderful. And then when Sventje came, well, it was even better. Two little children – my life was complete."

She talked about Sventje growing up. Sventje at school. Boys who liked Sventje (including a besotted teacher she'd *had to* have a talk with). Sventje's degree. Sventje's part-time job. Sventje's modelling.

I mentioned I found the self-orientation of her modelling

unhealthy. Her still living at home too.

"But what will happen if Sventje goes to England," she blurted, missing the point, breaking down again, "and gets married, has babies, and then there is a divorce?"

It was hard not to smile at the triple jump of unlikely events.

"But Mrs S, that's not the case," I reassured. "Sven has said she could never live in England. And there are plenty of English and American companies in Holland. Maybe I can work for one."

"Really, Scott? Really? Oh, please – please, please, please!"

She burst into tears again, this time whooping with joy between the sobs. Eventually, she puffed out her cheeks and lolled her tongue like a panting dog. It had been quite a morning. But the storm had broken.

"But Scott," she resumed, regaining her composure. "Why is Sventje so important to you?"

"Well," I relented, "she is everything."

I listed her qualities, mentioning beauty last. It wasn't so bad sharing my feelings. Even so, the mother now knew more about them than Sventje. And could relay them to the father, who might not welcome them quite as much, given his acidic performance the night before.

The telephone rang. It was Sventje. The mother spoke gently, her voice back to the candyfloss of the day before, as if nothing untoward had happened. She said Sventje had passed her viva and wanted me to come and celebrate in Utrecht, then passed the receiver, raising a finger to her lips. I nodded, yet it didn't feel right. Sventje was my girl, there were no secrets between us. And hostess or not, who was the mother to tell me what to do?

The train was hot and airless. I sat down, hands on knees, staring into space like an astronaut ready for take-off, my destination in someone else's hands. People stood about the platform, then drifted past while standing still. Gradually, sun-drenched orchards flitted by in regimental rows, like war graves, before giving way to flat field after flat field of grazing cows.

I did not look for woods where we might make love, but returned the blank stares, each cow unperturbed by the hot flash of yellow thundering past. For them, it was no different from the flash ten minutes ago, or in ten minutes' time, all part of the man-made landscape at the point where their field met the sky. Occasionally, a tail would swish away a fly or arch like an old-style pump to dispense dollops of shit; a head would look up at nothing in particular or rotate like a prop forward settling into a scrum. And that was it. That was their day.

If only I was a calf. I wouldn't have to think, or deal with a girl's parents. I could grow into a bull without the bullshit I'd just come through. Leave my mother when it was time. At least know where I stood. In a field mainly.

Hell, what had happened back there? I'd never felt comfortable with her profusion of cooked breakfasts, and had sensed something was up the moment she insisted I have one, as if compiling a dossier on her largesse as a hostess and my ingratitude as a guest. And then the inquisition itself, how she'd not listened to a word, before protesting a little too much. It was so two-faced. And now such a no-win situation. After all I'd done to win Sventje, and tried to do for her too. But had the mother been prying – or setting me up to fall, like a baited bear?

Either way, I couldn't have gone on the way things were, with her sniping behind Sventje's back. And maybe it was better to have things out in the open, forcing Sventje to move on.

But what jarred was the mother weeping, *It is so sad*. The way she shook her head too, as if in bitter disagreement with *it*. What was *it*, exactly? That we would end? If so, who had determined that? Not her, evidently. Or Sventje either. That meant it could only have been the father.

But this was not possible. Only the previous evening, he'd declared, *Englischman, I like you – you make me dink*, after I'd tried to impress him with my Law and Economics. Though he'd switched tack at dinner after I'd beaten him in an argument over Europe, turning to joke to the others in Dutch, his furtive eyes darting back to sneer at me, left out in the cold.

Had he taken umbrage at being upstaged by a student? Or had I got him wrong? Certainly it was strange how Sventje became another person around him. Red-faced. Silent. Uptight. Maintained he was *always right*. Had sent me that poem about prejudice.

Strange too about his other women. Who were they – office girls, prostitutes even? And how did this womanising or exploitation square with his lofty espousals of equality for women?

I remembered how Andre had once criticised him for having women "here and there"; the father had tutted in disapproval, and I'd not known where to look, thinking the outburst was due to Andre's alleged mental condition. Yet it was surely significant the attempt had taken place after a family meal: maybe the father had not simply taken a swipe at him for flunking university and becoming a car salesman, but Andre had just found out about his infidelities and no longer saw him as such a great god.

I shut my eyes at the many-headed monster before me, the collision of tectonic plates groaning in my ears.

I was out of my depth. And had never felt more alone.

Thank God I was going to see Sventje. Sweet, beautiful Sventje. The love of my life. How I wanted to hold her, and be held by her, to forget today had ever happened.

Should I tell her though? I'd promised not to, but would the mother refrain from telling the father? No chance. At least Sventje would see I'd had no motive to start the argument. Wouldn't she?

But what should I tell her? And what about the father's other women? Did she know about them already, or was I going to have to break that to her as well? How would she take it; what would she make of it all?

And what would the mother say? Tell the truth or downplay some things, exaggerate others – lie, even – to milk the situation and poison her daughter's mind against me? And if there was a discrepancy in accounts, who would Sventje believe? A strange relative or a relative stranger?

The train slowed into the station, and there she was, brimming with excitement among friends, searching for me in the carriage windows. But I drew back, wanting to carry on to the coast and into the sea – to submerge under the waves and return to England. I needed to cool down and work things out, not a party.

I met her friends, then walked with Sventje to a Thai restaurant by the canal. The green water drizzled with reflections of the lights from bars; trees smothered the buildings above, the leaves already rimmed with brown.

"You know," she confided, squeezing my hand, "I always wanted to come here with someone special."

I told her about the earlier interrogation and the damnation the day before, suggesting the mother was trying to nip it in the bud – but that Sventje should talk with her to get a balanced view. She listened in silence, eyes open wide.

"She had no right," she concluded at length, already agreeing with everything I'd said.

Back at the house, the mother acted normally, cooly. I went to sit by the father reading *De Telegraaf* by the piano, looking immaculate in his blazer, flannels and tie. At the kitchen table, the mother began cooing to Sventje, the magic of their fairy club still intact.

"And how goes it vid you?" He asked in a matter-of-fact way, with a cold glance over his gold half-moons.

"OK," I replied, unsure if my vow of silence extended to him as well.

"You vant a drink?" He demanded, eyes giving nothing away. "Beer, vine, someding else?"

"Yes," I hesitated, uneasy with his clinical hospitality. "White wine please. Thank you."

He flapped the broadsheet shut, tossed it on his chair and went to the fridge, slippers shishing across the wooden herringbone floor. Was he too now gearing up to take me down on a charge of insubordination?

"Did you hear about what happened here earlier?" I probed on his return, in need of an objective view.

"Yes, yes," he reported dismissively, handing me the glass then sitting down to rustle the paper open. "My vife and I have had a discussion."

So she hadn't kept her word either. But what had she told him? And did he now think I knew too much?

"Well," I writhed. "Every story has two sides, you know."

"Yes," he snapped, holding the paper wide open, screening me from view. "But she is your hostess and you are our guest. Derefore ve must give you a second chance."

Hold on. That meant I'd done something wrong – and she hadn't.

"Well, I'm not sure you've got the ethos of the situation right – "

"Edos is a padetic vord!" he retorted, his voice a super-power crushing a third world state.

I paused. It seemed whatever I said would only provide proof of some fault for use at a later date. His finality was closing out more sky.

"Well, maybe I should write down my version of events."

"Yes, yes," he trailed off, flicking the drooping paper straight. "I vould be interested to see dat."

His tone and manner showed he'd have no interest whatsoever.

There was a shriek of dismay from the table. The mother dashed out, followed by Sventje, face flushed. I looked on aghast. The father held the paper to one side and peered towards the door as footsteps clomped upstairs. He then looked back at me and sat forward a little.

"Look, don't vorry," he imparted, my friend again. "I dink maybe it vas all a misunderstanding."

Thank God. Such clashes must be commonplace. But at least he was on my side. Wasn't he?

The light was out in Sventje's room when I entered. There was a muffled sniffle in the darkness.

"Sven," I whispered, sliding onto the bed to lie behind her, "you OK?"

She didn't stir. I reached for her right shoulder.

"Fuck you!" she blasted, jerking her elbow backwards into my jaw.

I reeled from the blow, my bottom lip numb.

"What was that for?" I gawked. "What's wrong?"

"*What's wrong?* Huh!"

All the lovely tenderness of our perfect courtship was

draining away.

"Why? What did she say?"

"It's not what she said that matters," she complained. "It's that I left her crying. That's what matters."

Who cries wins, then. It was as simple as that in Sventje's little world. How absurd. I'd lost the girl – to her mother – but if I could turn on the waterworks, I'd be home and dry.

What a pity we hadn't met Katherijne in Delft on Tuesday. Kathy wouldn't be tethered to a parental home, living at the beck and call of elders who always knew best. Nor would she have such a naïve, inflated view of her parents and career, or stand for any of this nonsense. She'd establish the facts, work things out then sternly tell the mother this was the man she loved, finger wagging. And ask Andre outright why he'd tried what he had – and to hell with any directives that the question was out of the question.

It was no good thinking about Katherijne now though. I had to do something.

Or did I? This was Sventje's home. Sventje's mother. Sventje's father. Sventje's decision to live here, a passenger in her own life. This was Sventje's problem, then.

"What have you done, Scott," she implored, "to my poor, sweet mother?"

Indeed. What had I done to her? And would Sventje have described her as *poor* and *sweet* if she'd seen her in action earlier, or the day before? And what about *us* – didn't that come in to this at all?

"Well, perhaps it'd be better if I left then."

I moved to get up, but was immediately knocked sideways in an earth-shattering tackle.

"No, don't go, Scott," she splurged, arms clasped around me. "Please."

The reversal was astounding. Which way would she sway

tomorrow, or when I'd left for England – once the parents had honed their narratives, and got their hooks into her? There'd be no admission of any fault or the order not to plan my life around Sventje, just a disapproving verdict to sow doubt in her mind: *Look how he shouted and swore, after all we did for him – after all we've done for you. It is your choice, but he has no interest in your independence, career. And the English speak one language only and are not committed to Europe; he could never work in Holland. Where would he live, what would he do? It is only first love. You will meet someone better. We only want what's best for you.*

"You must stay," she gushed, "I need you. Nobody has ever been as kind to me as you."

An exaggeration, surely. But right now I'd take it.

She knelt over me, planting kisses around my neck.

Oh God. *I love you, Sventje.* Say it, you fool, say it.

But somehow, now, I couldn't.

Acknowledgements

My Brothers Would Kill You was first published in *Fiction On The Web*, February 2023. *Exposure* was first published in *Dreamcatcher* magazine issue no. 44, June 2021. *The Evil One* was first published in *Shorts* magazine, Winter edition, February 2023. *The Other Side* was first published in *Idle Ink* magazine, March 2023. *Sam* was first published in *Scribble* magazine issue no 99, Autumn 2023. *Surviving Larkin* was first published in *Sarasvati* magazine issue no 069, March 2023. *Making It Happen* was first published in *Steel Jackdaw* magazine edition 10, April 2023. *Not That Yellow Vincent* was first published in *Fruit* magazine Edition no 6 (and an audio-clip made available), May 2023. *Seeing Him Again* was first published in *Dreamcatcher* magazine iss-ue no 46, March 2023. *That Friday* was first published in the book *Celebrating Elisabeth de Bièvre and John Onians in Words and Pictures*, October 2023.

Hell In The Afternoon was commended in the Beagle North Q3 Competition, November 2022. *How To Deal With A Dark Smoke Offence* was highly commended in the Wordsmiths Writing Competition 2021. *The Day I Met Vini Reilly* won the Cinnamon Press Short Story Prize 2016 and was first published in the subsequent anthology *The Day I Met Vini Reilly* (Cinnamon Press 2016). *To Die For* was shortlisted in the Christopher Assheton-Stones Memo-rial Short Story Competition 2022 and first published in the subsequent anthology *Everyone Has A Story.*

Thanks to Carole Bromley, Doreen Gurrey, Sue Cooper, Joanne Stryker, Paul, Liz, Richard, Sue, John K, Sibylle,

Patrick Lodge, John Billington, Dave Nick, the Keats-Shelley Memorial Association, the Arvon Foundation and Jamie McGarry.

And a special thanks to Jo Haywood, for her forensic attention to detail, and Gail Ashton for her outstanding insight and support, without which this publication would not have been possible.

Will Kemp, September 2023